Nicholas Salaman is in ⬛⬛⬛⬛⬛⬛⬛⬛⬛⬛⬛⬛⬛⬛ chord. He was born in Somerset, educated at Radley and Oxford and spent nearly twenty years as an advertising copywriter. He now spends his time variously between advertising, running a herb and spice company of which he is co-owner, and writing. He has written plays for the theatre and television. His earlier novels, *The Frights* and *Dangerous Pursuits*, have established him as an original talent and a writer to watch.

By the same author

Dangerous Pursuits
The Frights

NICHOLAS SALAMAN

Falling Apart

GRAFTON BOOKS

A Division of the Collins Publishing Group

LONDON GLASGOW
TORONTO SYDNEY AUCKLAND

Grafton Books
A Division of the Collins Publishing Group
8 Grafton Street, London W1X 3LA

Published by Grafton Books 1987

First published in Great Britain by
The Alison Press/Martin Secker & Warburg Ltd 1986

Copyright © Nicholas Salaman 1986

ISBN 0-586-07048-6

Printed and bound in Great Britain by
Collins, Glasgow

Set in Times

'. . . the centre cannot hold . . .'
'The Second Coming' W. B. Yeats

Prologue

I know that she is up there, alone, sitting in the flat above the surgery.

I see that the rent is paid, food regularly delivered. And sometimes when she has gone out for one of her walks – she favours the twilight evenings now that summer is round the corner – I nip upstairs and try to clean the place a little while she is out.

She makes no sign that she has received any of these attentions.

It cannot go on like this.

There is nothing I can do about it.

I make sure that we never meet; doubtless she does the same. A confrontation would be too distressing for both of us.

Since the course of reconstructive treatment I am giving you will occupy a number of visits, it will perhaps help to pass away the time as you sit in the chair with your mouth open and your organs of speech temporarily stopped, if I relate to you the story of Charlet. Some of it I know at first hand. The rest she told me in the greatest detail, in circumstances of particular poignancy, so that I feel that I experienced it with her.

I will occasionally fill in with a little guesswork as and when it seems necessary. This I am sure you will allow. I feel you are an understanding person. Indeed, only to someone whom I can think of as a friend would I relate matters of such a personal, such a delicate nature.

Even so, I am encouraged to learn that when this

course is finished, you will be returning to your own country. I will never see you again.

Let us to work then. You like the head-rest a little lower. So?

Open wide and relax. I think you will find it quite an interesting sensation. The worst you should experience, from time to time, is a little discomfort.

PART ONE

'They flee from me that sometime did me seek
With naked foot, stalking in my chamber.
I have seen them gentle, tame, and meek,
That now are wild, and do not remember
That sometime they put themselves in danger
To take bread at my hand; and now they range
Busily seeking with a continual change.'

'Remembrance' Sir Thomas Wyatt

1

The new Trainee Assistant Brand Manager turned in admiration as an attractive young woman, neatly dressed in a brown suit with an expensive cream silk shirt, came down the corridor carrying a briefcase and a retinue of young men, one of whom stopped to retrieve a paper that had fluttered from her hand.

'Who's that?' said the trainee to the slightly older young man who had been allotted to show him round.

'Forget it,' replied his companion. 'That's Charlet. No point in getting horny. She's not for you. She's Group Brand Manager. She can have anyone she likes in this place – or out of it for that matter. She'll be a Board Director in a couple of years. *And* she's only thirty-four. Fix your eyes on one of the computer programmers. They're always glad to exchange their floppy discs for a little bit of executive hardware.'

The young recruit to Fastfoods, one of the largest convenience and snack food conglomerates in the country, sighed and, following his tutor past the snack-station at the end of the passage – dispensing a selection of refreshments that few in the building would go near if there were any conceivable alternatives – glimpsed through a wilderness of open-plan partitionettes just such a pool of electronic operatives, lank-haired girls with eyes fixed on their screens and fingers fiddling at their keyboards as if they were fly-fasteners.

He shuddered and walked on, wondering what kind of underwear the goddess wore.

Later, loitering in the glass and aluminium vestibule under the watchful eye of Luddington, the Liftman, he did in fact see her walking across to the executive carpark stairway with a susurration of silk, followed by a maintenance man carrying a case of the Company's wine merchant's champagne.

This was the life that had lured him from the prospect of one day running his father's small packaging factory into the world of cut-throat marketing, big office politics, and the glamour of the Business News pages.

And Charlet herself, if she had known what was passing through the button-eyed junior's mind – which as a matter of fact she probably would've if she had noticed him, used as she was to the ocular lust of young men – would've agreed with him.

There was nothing she knew of that gave her greater pleasure – not even sex or stolen weekends in smart country hotels, not that the two were mutually exclusive – than being a successful executive in a successful company, admired by her peers, ogled by her inferiors, with the sweet ointment of stardom daily secreted, like the waterproof oils of a sea-bird, through the mysterious functions of success glands.

As she directed the loading of the champagne into her sports car, and drove off to her pied-à-tierre to meet her boyfriend, she felt she'd never been happier. Protected from any of the inevitable splinters of envy from the occasional colleague by the benevolence of Old Garramond, one of the architects of Fastfood's growth, who had always taken a particularly friendly interest in her, there was nothing that could go wrong.

A down-and-out drunk suddenly stepped out in front of her, gesticulating and shouting. 'Faaa . . .'

She swore, swerved, and watched him as he stood

there, arms lifted in some sort of red-biddied malediction, until he was no more than a spidery homunculus in her mirror, just a momentary smudge on a shining field of promise.

2

A couple of nights later, when she was coming home late after dinner with her friend, something rather odd happened.

He had dropped her off prudently a couple of streets away. One could never be too careful.

As she walked back along the familiar sidewalk, bright under the orange sodium lamps, she suddenly felt a great weight upon her, as if those orange clouds were actually pressing down with the full weight of Creation behind them.

She looked up the street in a sort of horizontal reflex from that great vertical pressure, and saw a motorbike coming towards her in the distance. As it approached, she suddenly knew that if she didn't hold her mind right or (as she put it to me later) hold it right in her mind, it would go off the road. It was as simple as that. There would be nothing left to hold it on the road

'That's crazy!' She spoke aloud to herself. It seemed that the act of speech might disperse some of the weight on her brain. 'You're not here to hold bikes on the road.'

So she let it go, or rather stopped holding it.

The motorbike took the bend with immaculate precision and passed on into the night.

For a moment she stood there, almost more shocked than if the bike really lay slewed across the grass verge beyond the tarmac, the lights coming on in neighbouring houses, and people appearing. She could almost hear the voices.

'My God, he's dead.'

'What happened?'

'I don't know. I was just walking past.'

There were no lights, no accident, no confusion. The accident was somehow in herself, going on in her mind, wheels spinning, its engine still miraculously running. Perhaps – the thought sped through her mind – it was not the bike at all, it was her. But it was nonsense, of course.

She turned and walked the last hundred yards or so to her home, her shoes making a brisk, sensible noise on the non-slip composition surface.

3

She undressed in the darkness though she knew her husband was awake.

'Good movie?' her husband asked.

'Great. Anthony Quinn was an animal.'

She had told him she was going to see the film *La Strada* at the Classic with her friend Poppy. She knew he couldn't stand Italian films, or Poppy. She had seen the film twice already.

'Then we had dinner at the Pulcinella. Pasta was the only thing after all that macho brutishness. Washed down with a little rough up-country wine.'

'I thought you had an early presentation tomorrow?'

'I do.'

'We don't want you late for your early presentation.'

'I know.'

Her husband was a designer of comic greeting cards, and worked at home. They had agreed she should go

14

back to her old job when the children were past kindergarten. It had all worked out rather well. She kicked her briefs away somewhere into the darkness, and reached under the pillow for her pyjamas.

'Aaaagh!'

There was something alive and cold under there and squirming, like a tubiform jelly.

'What's the matter?'

Lights came on down the passage from the direction of the children's rooms.

'It's only a poor old magic slippery worm,' he said mildly. 'I bought them at the Bazaar, and we've been playing with them all evening. One must've been left there by mistake, mustn't it children?'

Her husband had a taste for practical jokes which they all enjoyed, especially the children. They were standing there in the doorway, lit from behind like accusing angels.

'Yes, it must.'

They must all have been lying there, sleepless in the dark, waiting for her to come back.

A wriggly worm of unease stirred somewhere inside her.

'Back to bed now, kiddoes. Mummy's got an early presentation.'

'Not again.'

It was a purely ritual protest. They liked getting their own breakfast. They liked getting any meal for themselves except supper. Supper was down to their father. He was an expert cook, and encouraged the children to share his enthusiasm. It was kind of eerie to hear them discussing estouffade de veau à l'ancienne or the proper ingredients of béchamel sauce the way other kids talked about popcorn, but it kept them all happy, and meant she didn't have to cook. They even accompanied their father shopping, pressing the pears, sniffing the melons, like real little Escoffiers.

'Come on. Back to bed.'

'OK, OK. 'Night, Dad.'

'Good night, homunculi.'

'Don't I get a goodnight?' she asked.

'Oh all right. 'Night.'

She kissed them. They responded elusively, wriggling and flitting away down the corridor.

Just for a moment she debated with herself whether to tell Howard what she had seen on the way home, then remembered that she was supposed to have come from the other direction.

She got into bed, gave Howard a quick kiss, turned over, and lay staring at the hairline gap in the curtains where the moon used to shine before they put up the new street light.

4

She woke with an unusual sense of reluctance, and lay there watching her hand snatching about at the alarm-clock.

It always took her a minute or two to sort out her priorities when she woke up.

The first thing she thought of was a report that had been lying on her desk for a week. Curiously, she just couldn't seem to get around to doing it.

Then she remembered her strange premonition of last night. It triggered a little run of defensiveness. Could her imagination have been influenced by that brush with the tramp outside the office?

And then she thought, it's too trivial to waste time on. People are falling off their bikes all over the place; it's only natural to assume occasionally that they're going to do it in front of one.

At that point she remembered her presentation to the Plans Board. She had ninety minutes to get to the office.

She fixed her face and dressed with a sort of flowing urgency.

'Nice panties,' said her husband.

They were silk with little curlicues of lace.

'Glad you like them,' she said, buttoning a suit that combined efficiency with femininity.

'Are they for the benefit of the Plans Board?'

'Oh no,' she said lightly, 'they prefer the peek-a-boo variety.'

'Peek-a-boo,' said Howard. 'I like it. There must be a comic card there somewhere. Would one say peek-a-boo, do you think, to a goose?'

She felt that her panties had sustained the conversation for long enough. Actually they were for the benefit of her boyfriend.

'Must dash,' she said.

She ran downstairs, grabbed a cup of coffee and ran up again to collect her bag and say goodbye. Howard was still lying in bed.

'It's all right for some,' she said.

'Pentelle's coming today. She doesn't get here till ten. Can't get anything done till Pentelle arrives.'

Pentelle was the children's name for his part-time assistant. A short shy girl, with indecisive blue eyes.

'Shall we see you tonight?' he asked. 'We could have a feast.'

'Sorry, love. Got to go over to the agency. I'll probably snatch a bite with them.'

'Hope the Plans Board doesn't have a fit of peek,' he said.

'What?'

She was halfway out of the door.

'Nothing.'

'Oh for goodness sake . . .'

As she drove her little two-seater (a company car) out of the garage, her spirits rose. She enjoyed the image she would provide, bowling along with the top down. It was a fine morning. A light breeze stirred the shrubs on the estate and bowled the empty crisp packets down the walkways like little galleons.

She didn't take the car into the office every day. Only Directors had a reserved slot, the public park was expensive, and the morning traffic could be horrendous, but this morning she was early.

The road where the accident hadn't happened was one of her short cuts. She took it without thinking.

The scene was still so vivid in her mind that she almost expected to see the white tape stretched around the lamp-post and across part of the grass verge, the police car parked, and two policemen measuring the ground, the white cut-out in the shape of a sprawled figure lying at the foot of the lamp-post.

As she drove past, trying to look the other way, eyes seemed to follow her reproachfully, almost as if a notice, propped on a trestle, requested information about the accident.

She did not stop. What could she do?

5

There is a law that rules the naming of office blocks. The implications of the name are always in a directly inverse proportion to the character of the resident company.

The headquarters of United Fastfoods was called John Keats House. It was one of a number of blocks, each named after a poet, located in a rundown area of the city that had suddenly started to run up again. Of course, hardly anyone lived there now. It was all new offices, multi-storey carparks, and shopping precincts for non-residents.

Every morning, some six hundred people converged on the building at nine o'clock; vanished through its revolving jaws; ate, worked, fondled behind the filing cabinets, dreamed, despaired, floated along on automatic pilot; until the moment came to be ejected again, pale and partially digested, into the five o'clock evening. The lifts groaned continually in a windy lamentation for all the bright butterflies that were caught in the toils of the spider. It was a sound of infinite and unforgettable dreariness you quickly took for granted.

Fastfoods had been, under the former name of Butterby's, an old family firm making perfectly good though perhaps not very fashionable cookies until about six or seven years ago when the old dispensations began to change and the bottom dropped out of the biscuit tin. Nobody wanted boring cookies any more.

Just in time, however, the Company had attracted the notice of one of the new consortiums that were springing up all over the place. Butterby's profits might be poor but its reputation was good and its distribution could be trebled by being tied in with a larger group.

Old Garramond, the Chairman of Butterby's, was retained. He had a sound name in the business. But a new Managing Director from Maxi-Milk, called Affleck, was put in, and he embarked on a radical new product development programme. Affleck had hit upon a stratagem for putting the bloom back into the balance sheet with an idea which was breathtaking in its simplicity.

'Bubbles,' he said one day to a startled Board, 'think bubbles.'

They looked at each other, their faces registering a

19

spectrum of emotions. The newer men tried to express admiration and enthusiasm tinged with shrewdness, while at the same time unable actually to grasp what the Managing Director was on about, and keen that no one else should be seen to understand it first. The Marketing Director understood but resented the fact that the MD had appropriated an idea which, truthfully, they had hatched together. But some of the Directors were still of the older guard and simply did not understand what was going on.

Did he mean speech balloons, their eyes questioned each other, was this some kind of new advertising gimmick?

Sensing bemusement about him, the Managing Director smote the table with his fist.

'Bubbles are made of air. Air costs nothing. Surround your bubbles with a crispy crackly snappy crunchy integument and what do you have? A great big profit on every bag you sell.'

'But won't people mind buying practically nothing?' enquired one of the older Directors, either braver or more stupid than the rest.

The MD turned on him like a seraph of exposition, mentally putting him down as the next to go.

'Mr Lustard, you are not perhaps au fait with the latest market trends?'

Mr Lustard looked miserable. He had no idea of the latest anything, and wouldn't know a trend if it walked up to him and jabbed him with its pointed calf-length boots.

The MD strode over to a small cabinet which stood in the corner of the room, and fished out an armful of charts.

'If we extrapolate the Nielsen figures of the last five years and view them against the parameters of . . .'

And he went on to show that the housewife did not

wish her children to fill themselves up with stodge between meals but did want to stick something in their mouths so she could get on with living her life whatever that might be. What she wanted, in fact, was something light and tasty. Hence, the MD explained as if to a backward macaque, the philosophy of bubbles meant not simply a profitable flash in the pan, a one-off purchase, but a repeat-buying pattern that would make millions for the Company.

'And let us not confine ourselves to snack products,' he concluded. 'The bubble concept has applications in many different markets. Thus the nibble arena, though the object of our primary concentration, can be seen as but the spearhead for a more truly cosmic philosophy. A report, please, Mr Prelati.'

Mr Prelati, one of the new smooth-featured men, in due course obliged. Mr Lustard did indeed go, and many more like him, and it was fortunate for Charlet that all this was happening just as she was forming up to rejoin the firm after having a family. Frankly, if the old guard had still been in charge, there wouldn't have been a firm to rejoin.

Anyway, Old Garramond liked the look of her. He somehow saw her as a Butterby's person succeeding in the new dispensation. Though basically against women in business, he nevertheless could appreciate the advantages of having this girl on the Marketing side. It was modern. It was go-ahead. And, after all, women represented 75 per cent of the market.

Besides she had good legs.

Charlet, after a spell catching up with the changes in the business since she had last worked, enjoyed finding that she was more than a match for most of the men, even the new ones the Managing Director was getting in, with too much white of the eyes showing, and a tendency to enthuse about in-store sampling.

The thing was, the men seemed terribly nervous about actually taking a decision.

Affleck had impressed upon them all that, at this stage of Fastfoods' development, the Company could not afford to be seen to make mistakes in the market place. It would rock the confidence of the trade in the successful lines they had created.

The result was that a number of executives stopped making any decisions at all. However, this too excited Affleck's censure. He believed in new product development, and he wished to see evidence of activity.

In truth, Affleck had been promoted beyond his capacity to inspire those under him. Indeed, he actually enjoyed the fact that many of the male executives couldn't get the hang of what he wanted at all. It made him feel good.

Charlet, almost without thinking, discovered a natural aptitude for the game.

The Plans Boards were a case in point.

To regulate developments within the Company, and to make sure he had every pie at his fingertips, Affleck had instituted a system of review committees which were composed of various directors and managers, research people and money men, all convened at certain well-defined intervals (and sometimes with terrible suddenness).

These were the Plans Boards, and this was where Charlet really shone.

There were so many of them. There was a Plans Board for new products, a Plans Board to monitor advertising campaigns, a Plans Board to sample competitors' lines, a Plans Board to review the year's Plans Boards.

Because they were so dull, it was nice to have a girl around, so she got invited to sit on rather more than would normally have come her way as an Assistant Brand Manager.

And in almost all of them – perhaps because she was married, wasn't afraid of getting fired, felt she had nothing to lose – Charlet was the one who seemed to have the temper of decision.

It was the MD's favourite phrase.

'Don't tell me if he's got a good brain,' he would say. 'Don't tell me if he's lucky. What I want to know is, has he got the temper of decision?'

Her promotion was rapid. From Assistant Brand Manager, she became Brand Manager with responsibility for Lanterns. Admittedly it was one of the less fancied brands, a bit of a flyer, a soy and noodle-flavoured bubble about to be launched in one of the backwoods TV areas, not really expected to go anywhere; so with few impediments to its progress, and with her decisive approach and particularly with her advertising campaign based on a line of her own: 'Lanterns. They're light the way you like,' she had soon built it up into a substantial business.

It had become a national brand, with unprecedented speed. From then on, she became known as someone to be watched, as near stardom as you could get in Fastfoods.

Her next promotion was up to Assistant Group Brand Manager. She should have stuck at this level for at least three years, but she had a stroke of luck.

Her new boss fell ill the very day she joined him. She had to take over the whole job herself with a new man under her while her boss was away sick. It was serious. He never came back. The world was her shellfish-flavoured Sea-Snack, or so her new assistant told her over a glass of champagne at the Wine Bar.

Of course, her home life suffered, but to be honest she had never found home really satisfying. Her husband and the children formed a unit without her. She always had the feeling that she didn't quite belong, or that she belonged if she wasn't there too much. She was fond of them all in a way, but an important part of her life lay outside them. She couldn't explain it. She felt they understood.

Of course, working with so many men, admired and flattered, flirted with and lusted after, it was inevitable that she should have an affair.

The first, it turned out, was with her new assistant, Larry, a personable and even rather glamorous young man who had been a very minor star on the international tennis circuit. Love didn't come into it on her part. She wanted him for the excitement of it. There were some indications that he felt rather more deeply about her, which she tried to discourage.

It was, as it happened (or was it another of her well-tempered decisions?), a sound career move since it cemented their working relationship and allowed ideas to develop laterally, out of hours.

'It gives a whole new meaning to the expression "being on the job",' she heard someone say about them, but it was with envy rather than malice.

The affair hadn't lasted more than a year. He had been transferred to a more senior Group with more responsibility. She had felt it was better to wind down the relationship. There could well have been conflicts of interest.

They were still good friends.

As it happened, he was a member of the Plans Board that had gathered in Meeting Room 16 to hear her survey on New Product projects that might be undertaken to fill the number 3 factory's excess capacity on a short-to-medium-term basis.

They smiled at each other when she arrived, only marginally late, and he made his way over to greet her.

'Have lunch with me today?'

'Oh, Larry, I've a report to finish. Can it wait?

'Hm hm.'

He shook his head mysteriously.

'All right. But it'll have to be quick.'

'Gianni's at one.'

They were interrupted by the Plans Board Chairman, a new man called Foxworth, Marketing Manager of Confectionery and Snacks Division, who rapped on the table for attention.

'Gentlemen, before we hear uh Charlet's presentation,' he observed the Company rule, wherever possible, of using Christian names to make it seem like a happy family, but he obviously didn't like it, 'I would just like to read you a memo sent me by the MD reaffirming the New Product philosophy to which he is committed. Its theme, as you will see, is that the bubble revolution is not happening fast enough. It is headed "Crunchtime" . . .'

They had heard it all before. It wasn't easy to transform a range that had its roots in shortbread and gingernuts into no-substance snackings, and, as it happened, Charlet's contribution to the corporate shift did nothing to help. It wasn't her fault. She had been given erroneous information on the technical ability of the plant in question. It could only accept freeze-dried or granulated powders for puffing. It could not cope with semi-liquids.

It wasn't her fault, but it shouldn't have happened. She was responsible; like the captain of a ship, the presentation lay under her command.

Finally, the Chairman stopped her, almost in mid-sentence

'We're wasting our time. We will have to reconvene next month. Drop a fucking missile on whoever supplied that information, would you, Charlet? It's page one stuff, you know. The whole production line would caramelize. Of course, it's one way of dealing with excess capacity.'

There was a general laugh at her expense. She had not got so far so quickly without making enemies.

'No blame attaches itself to you,' he concluded in a manner which suggested the opposite. She felt herself blushing.

She wished the man would stop staring at her through his impenetrable steel-rimmed glasses as though he could see into her knickers. She had whiled away many a dull presentation with vaguely similar speculations about her colleagues, but in this instance his attention seemed brutish and uncouth.

She wished she hadn't found it, at the same time, just a little exciting. She had noticed that his particular trick was almost never to smile except when he was being offensive. It had a curious effect on those around him, persuading them that he must be a very serious and promotable person. She experienced a small intimation that it might be something of a challenge.

6

Lunch was really her favourite time, neither work nor home. It appealed to her sense of not belonging.

Of course, there were many occasions when it had to be a working lunch, shrink-wrapped sandwiches and diet lager in the meeting room or grander affairs in one of the luncheon booths in the Directors' Restaurant with prawn cocktails, chicken and Chablis. When the boat was really being pushed out, there could even be the ultimate luxury of a table in one of the gilded haunts that had opened in the district as a result of the rise of the office blocks, places like La Gioconda or Il Palazzo dei Medici, pink-napkined, softly lit, and redolent of joyless swilling.

There was also the staff canteen which provided lavish helpings of almost well-cooked food but no alcohol, and huge blown-up pictures of lakes and larch trees, not very clean, and in black and white.

The best way to spend lunch, however, was to go to one of the older darker Italian dives that still survived like tiny scurrying mammals under the feet of the new concrete dinosaurs.

It was in one of these that Charlet found Larry. He was already sitting there, sipping a Campari next to a sweet trolley.

Men's glances flickered towards her as she made her way across the room.

'Sorry I'm late,' she said, 'I was just trying to get a little work in on that report I'm doing. I just can't seem to get my ass in gear over that thing.'

She enjoyed using vigorous masculine terms. It gave them a new pungency when they emerged from a pretty mouth, she had been told.

'Think nothing of it,' said Larry, 'I'd wait twice as long for someone half as good-looking.'

He seemed to have been taking lessons in charm from someone. After they had exchanged a little of the half intimate, half joshing banter that ex-lovers on good terms reserve for one another, he said something else that surprised her.

'It's good to get out of the good old glass and concrete, isn't it, and to be actually sitting in brick? Brick gives you the feeling that the ground might still be alive underneath it. Have you any idea what time of year it is?'

'Don't be silly. What are you talking about?'

'It could be spring. It could be anything. Up there,' he nodded in the direction of John Keats House, 'it's always any time. Even walking over here. No fallen leaves. No smell of bonfires. We could be in a blister. We could be underwater. Or in a cyst on Mars. We make bubbles in a blister on Mars.'

'Are you all right, Larry?'

She hadn't heard him talk like this before. It disturbed her, made her feel uncomfortable.

'I'm going to leave Fastfoods.'

This was better. She'd heard him say that many times. She knew he couldn't. His appetite for money was a joke between them. Somehow, though, this time it sounded more desperate.

'I shall start a tennis school,' he began, 'in the sun.'

'Or design golf courses.'

'Or run an up-market bordello.'

'After a morning like that, I'm half inclined to join you,' she joked.

'It'd be great. Though I'm not sure that Harriet would like that.'

'Harriet?'

That wriggly worm of unease again. Ridiculous, of course. It wasn't as if she were having an affair any more with Larry. But she felt a perceptible lurch of misgiving, misgiving yes, and perhaps jealousy. Had she misjudged him all this time? She hadn't wanted him in the end, but she didn't want anyone else to have him. Was that it? Or was there something more to him that only now was she beginning to value?

'Harriet's my fiancée. That's what I was going to say.'

'Terrific.' She took a mouthful of vodka and tonic. 'Tell me about it.'

While he was going through the various aspects of Harriet's divinity, she waited impatiently, only half concentrating on the litany. Tennis, golf, cooking, elegance, intellect, charm . . . Harriet appeared to have the lot. Finally the catalogue seemed to be complete.

'That's fantastic, Larry,' she said. 'I'm so happy for you. Listen. There's one thing I wanted to ask you about.'

And she was just about to recount the strange event of the evening before when a shadow fell across their table.

It was the Divisional Marketing Manager, Bruce Foxworth. The last person she wanted to tell about an experience so elusive, so mockable. There was something loud and a little dangerous about him, as though he hadn't been properly house-trained. Though lean and tall, he seemed to have a girth, a dimension of energy, even violence. He was like a thin man with a fat man struggling to get out. He sat himself down at their table, seizing a passing waiter and ordered saltimbocca.

'I just snuck out for a beer and a sandwich,' he said, helping himself to their wine, 'when I see you guys fornicating in a corner. Listen, Charlet, I hear you're late with that report. I hope you can afford the time to sit here stuffing your pretty face with tortelloni in the company of this shmuck.'

How was it everyone suddenly seemed to know about that report? Charlet began to feel like a rabbit in front of a car. For some reason, the man had that effect on her. She felt, for once, absurdly powerless in the face of his crass masculinity. She had the feeling that at any moment he would, he could, destroy her. It was a sensation she had never experienced before.

'Larry tells me he's getting married,' she countered, energetically. 'Isn't that terrific?'

'It's terrific if it means he's not monopolizing you. Larry, is this true? Waiter, some more wine . . .'

She walked back later with Larry, leaving the Marketing Manager tucking in to a massive mound of profiteroles.

'You ought to come out with me some time, dinner maybe, and I'll give you something really special. You like Turkish cooking? Meanwhile, don't sit on that report. If you want to sit on anything you can sit on my bicycle,' was his parting shot.

'That man has all the charm of a ballistic missile,' said Larry when they were almost out of earshot.

They walked on a little. The indeterminate sunshine glowered from a thousand windows on to the concrete bowls of late geraniums.

'I was going to say . . .' they both exclaimed together.

'After you . . .' she said.

She didn't really know what she was going to say. The man Foxworth had opened up in her a little warren of self-doubts.

'I was going to say,' said Larry, 'the other place she's really good is, you know, bed. I know you don't think that's so important but for me it's . . . well it's important . . . she's a tremendously . . . giving person.'

He hadn't meant it as a slight, but it piqued her. She actually quite enjoyed the notion of bed. The truth was, she had found, that Larry himself (like many over-goodlooking men) had a somewhat hokey-cokey attitude to sex which had done little to excite her.

'That's terrific. I'm so happy for you, Larry,' she said.

'Actually,' he said, 'I can't afford to leave Fastfoods just yet. I was only kidding. Harriet is a single parent. I'm lobbying for Nut Puffs in my new group, and then I can form up for a rise.'

Nut Puffs was the most important single development in the last three years, he told her. He'd just got wind of it from a chum in Special Projects which Foxworth had been heading, where you could lose your job if you broke security.

He asked her not to breathe a word to anyone. She promised that of course she wouldn't, he didn't even need to mention it.

7

At work that afternoon, she still couldn't get down to the report.

As she sat at her executive desk, with the view of the run-down city regenerating itself below her, bulbs of glass, webs of steel and concrete, a whole anti-nature sprouting and pullulating in the squashy hinterland of what had once been markets and warehouses, she felt like that rabbit on the road. Her mind was full of thought but her pen-arm was powerless. Foxworth loomed, steel-rimmed spectacles flashing. There was nothing she could do. Silly of evolution to make adrenalin so paralysing.

Her mind kept turning back to the previous night. Perhaps it had been, after all, a crazy premonition brought on by the demanding James, her current boyfriend. Really, he was enough to induce an aberration of some kind.

No doubt it was partly down to his wife. He had told her about his wife over many dinners. It was almost a bond between them, how different his wife was.

She was elegant, highly strung, good company on a good day, an excellent cook.

They had no children.

'You're my baby,' James's wife used to say to him (on a good day).

If she really thought so, incest was clearly her thing, since it was sex, Charlet sensed, that really held them together. Sex and its Permanent Under Secretary, guilt. She made him pay for his pleasure by means of emotional blackmail.

She was jealous, James said. Not that ordinary jealousy

which is like the benign side of pain, a sign either of true love, or that something's going wrong which can perhaps be corrected. No, this was diseased jealousy, a kind of hyper-sensitive oscillator that would go off like a car-alarm at the veriest hint, the merest sparrow's fart of opportunity. Or even sometimes at nothing at all. You could never tell with James's wife.

Once triggered, if it were at a party for instance, she would play up monstrously with other men, or indeed with other women. James had on one occasion found her canoodling with a dusky model among the fur coats in their hosts' bedroom.

When they got away, the scene would start in earnest.

'What the hell d'you think you were doing?' she would demand.

'I don't know what you mean.'

'Oh yes you fucking do. I could see you. You were drooling at that girl, staring down at her tits. I could see your erection from across the room.'

'She was just a friend of my brother's. We were talking about tennis.'

'Tennis my backside.'

At that point he might be able to deflect her if he wasn't too drunk. (James liked to drink.)

'Yes,' he would say, 'it does look good in a short white skirt.'

And she might laugh.

And then she might not. In which case the row would thunder through the night and on into the following day, and night, and day, and then, after maintaining a Gehenna-like silence, she would announce an armistice by suddenly responding to one of his peaceable gestures. They would make the quarrel up – she loved the making up – and then they would have rapturous snorty sex, and live in a state of unbalanced affection until the next thunderbolt descended.

James was infuriated with his wife. He knew the marriage should be over. But still he couldn't leave her (if he suggested it, she countered with a suicide threat). Which made him need Charlet all the more. It was, he said, as vicious as a circle could get.

Charlet knew that she, in her turn, should call the thing off, but every time she got around to saying it, he'd telephone her next day at work, leave flowers in reception, whisk her off to a champagne dinner, make passionate love to her in the Waiting Room (their name for her pied-à-terre in town), and so the whole circus would begin again.

She felt safe with men who were weaker than her, but she liked them to be enterprising, and James was certainly that. It had been his adrenalin, perhaps derived from his relationship with his wife, that had kept their affair zapping along. But today she felt differently. It was time perhaps for a change. She would tell him this evening.

'Charlet. Charlet.'

Someone was standing in front of her waving a file and flashing his headlights. It was the man Foxworth. She had known he would appear. She felt again that strange and alarming combination of fear and attraction.

'The report, Charlet. How much longer are you going to sit on that pretty ass of yours?'

'Sorry, Bruce.' She mustered an aloof smile. 'I didn't think it was actually wanted till next week.'

'It's wanted yesterday.'

'Oh. Well, I think somebody could have told me, don't you? Look. Here's the memo about it. It says the 17th. As for my pretty ass, as you call it, don't you think that smacks of sexism?'

Foxworth seemed not in the least impressed with her filing system or her resort to sexual politics. He leant over her menacingly.

'Don't you ever,' he said, 'don't you ever bandy bits of

paper with me again. As for sexism, I'll smack your ass right out of a job if you give me that sixth-hand feminist cowshit ever again.'

'Oh,' she said, seizing up and just sitting there.

'That's all right, then,' he said. 'Dinner Monday night?'

A vestige of pride and self-preservation made her resist quite such an outrageously confident take-over.

'No,' she said abruptly, 'I'm busy.'

'You're damn right you are,' he replied, 'you're busy finishing the report by Monday evening. Then I take you out to dinner.'

'I'll see,' she said, disturbingly tempted. 'I really don't know.'

But he was already halfway out of the room, shouting for Herbert Loach down the corridor.

In a panic the like of which she hadn't known since she was twelve and struggling with logarithms, with the remains of the inedible school lunch in a hanky up her knicker-leg, she somehow managed to patch together a few pages on the wretched report, but they were way below her normal standard.

Her efforts to provide a quick résumé and recommendations for action weren't helped by the image of Jamie already there in the Waiting Room, pacing and fidgeting and getting just a little drunk on her supply of Château Cantemerle.

It would make it just that bit more difficult to say to him what she had in mind.

8

It had a floor of highly polished wood, with one or two strategically placed rugs, and wooden furniture designed to offend no one.

There was a tiny kitchen, a bedroom just big enough for the bed, and this strange shiny sitting-room where you expected the nurse to come in at any moment and call you in for an extraction.

Some of her male colleagues, she knew, who lived out of town also had places in the city where they conducted their affairs, slept when they had an early meeting, or simply got away from their families.

It had seemed to her an admirable idea. Not that she often wanted to spend a whole night away from home; but somewhere to go to after work, have a drink, maybe a meal, make love, talk over the day, it was the civilized way to behave.

Some time previously, when she'd taken a wristwatch to be repaired by an old man Larry had told her about, she had seen a notice advertising a flat in the next block. It was over a dentist's. When she looked round, she hadn't, of course, exactly fallen in love with it; but it was convenient, and modestly priced.

She had told Larry about it, and they had debated why it was so cheap.

'Perhaps the dentist has something to hide,' suggested Charlet.

'He sells replacement mandibles to a body bank and conceals his jawless victims under the floorboard,' said Larry.

'He gives girls laughing gas and does terrible things with his polisher.'

'His nurse is a monster who has him under her thumb.'

'Literally.'

It turned out that many people were put off by the proximity of the surgery, according to the agent, an ingratiating man with a presumptuous candour. The drill could set up sympathetic vibrations. Some people had a fear of dentists, he whispered confidentially, as if imparting a truth not generally known.

However, since she was only there after six o'clock, it didn't worry her at all. She took the place (though she didn't tell her husband). There seemed no point.

She never saw the dentist or his nurse, so whatever went on down there, it was discreet. The rest of the building consisted of offices or studios. In the evening, the Waiting Room was like a little polished dinghy of frivolity in a sea of seriousness.

After Larry, she had one or two less important affairs – not too many, that would have been lacking in style – but enough to keep her in touch without damaging her reputation.

When she did sleep out, she found herself doing it with younger men. You could smell the disappointment in older guys, they were more interesting but less bouncy. They were losing their elastic. So, on the three-day seminars and the Area Sales Conferences, she would drink and dance in the evening with the older men, and sleep with an Assistant Brand Manager at night. The older man would be tired or not want to be put to the test because he would be too full of guilt and drink to get it up. The younger man would be shy and grateful – at least, the ones she chose would be, and not too bothered when it didn't work out longer term, which it didn't.

So she had gone on. Successful at work, removed by a millimetre of transparent cladding from her home by the sense that it wasn't maybe the most important thing in her life, yet without any particular sense of what that might be, and getting (though she wouldn't admit it to herself) just a little bored. Was this what independence and profit-sharing was about?

It was at this point that she met James at a Food Trade Fair.

Fastfoods, naturally, had a stand at which she was playing hostess with one or two of her Brand Managers. She saw him inspecting their Snackerjacks with what looked like almost moronic interest, and she stepped out and offered him one to try before the Promotion dolly could get to him. Somehow she liked the look of him – slightly balding, not particularly tall, neither fat nor thin, with an expression in no way distinguished but with a certain humorous deprecation about it as though the world couldn't really be this absurd. (She discovered later, of course, that this mocking air was only a front – his detachment was entirely superficial.)

He had taken the Snackerjack she extended towards him, with the serious consideration of a gourmet.

He had sniffed it. He had brushed its surface with his finger, and licked it. Finally, he had taken a tiny bite, and eaten it with little quick nibbling motions, pausing to sloosh it round his mouth like a wine taster. Then suddenly he went to a waste-bin and spat the whole thing out with an expression of the utmost revulsion.

Charlet was almost sick with laughter. Her colleagues normally treated the Company's products with exaggerated respect. Anything less would not have helped one's prospects of advancement. But it was refreshing, almost revelatory, to see a normal human reaction for a change.

'You don't like the new Pork 'n' Beans flavour?' she enquired.

'It tastes like a brittle fart.'

It was not an inaccurate assessment.

'One does not knock the Product,' she said.

Afterwards when they were in bed in his hotel room, making love for the second time, she made one of those little slooshing gurgles which not even the most polished executive can provide without some kind of temporary embarrassment, and he had paused in his lovemaking, kissed her, and said: 'Now if Fastfoods could make a bubble like that, they could cut their advertising budget and corner the market tomorrow.'

She had almost loved him then for turning her embarrassment into a joke, but she was quite sure she didn't love him now, a year later.

A joke was a great way to start an affair but it was like a diet of Snackerjacks by itself – too thin for nourishment. The sense of humour in the end didn't seem to make up for James's high state of strung-up-ness, the endless quarrels, and make-ups and inconclusive returnings to the status quo. Perhaps, the thought used to strike her, the tension in his household wasn't all of his wife's making.

When Charlet finally arrived that evening, she was annoyed with herself for being late, irritated at having put off, once again, that bloody report, and cross with James for looking sulky. However, he poured her a drink and they both sat down. He was playing music that particularly annoyed her, a sort of drivelling but noisy modern jazz. To shut it out, she started to tell him about her experience the previous night. In relating it, even while she spoke, she was aware that she couldn't expect anyone else to feel deeply about a non-event like that. It was one of those personal things.

He was not unkind though.

'You're imagining it,' he said, 'we all have moments like that. You mustn't get delusions of responsibility.'

'I know but . . .'

'What you need's another drink. A touch of the blushful . . .'

She noticed that he was slightly drunk. He had been slightly drunk quite a bit recently.

'How did the presentation go?' he enquired, in the manner of one who wants to be asked about his own day.

'So so.'

She didn't like to admit a reverse. In her desire to change the subject, however, she made another error.

'Oh, by the way, I had lunch with Larry,' she said. Then remembering James's highly developed powers of jealousy: 'He wanted to talk about the Nut Puff launch.'

'Just so long as you didn't do more than that. A little private function upstairs in the Grotto Blu Room? A little needle nighdle noodle?'

She could feel him teetering on the verge of truculence, so she eased back a little. She didn't feel like a row.

'Tell me about your day,' she asked him.

'It wasn't my day, it was my night.'

So that was it. His wife was giving him a hard time.

'Oh dear. Not again.'

'You can say not again. You don't have to go through it.'

'Couldn't you just sleep in the spare room?' she asked pacifically.

'You're just like Bunny,' replied James insensately. 'I try to explain, I suppose it's too much to hope for sympathy but all I get is argument.'

Who or what was Bunny? She almost asked, but felt that enlightenment would be unrewarding.

She breathed deeply, and said: 'All right. Tell me about it.'

'And there's something else. I think Susie's following me.'

'She's following you?'

'Having me followed.'

39

'Not here?'

She felt a trace of alarm. She didn't like the thought of cold unseen eyes on her. That wife Susie – it seemed you could never be quite sure she wouldn't get up to something completely deranged. She appeared to have no sense of dignity. Or was she running mad, a sort of suburban Lizzie Borden? Or was it all James's fantasy?

'I think she's found out about you. There was a dreadful scene.'

'Why don't you just move in here?'

She didn't in the least want him to, but of course she knew he wouldn't. Indeed, she already knew what his answer would be. She just wanted to hear him say it again.

'I've thought about that,' he told her seriously. 'But she'd kill herself if I left her.'

Originally it had been almost painful, certainly irritating, to learn. Now it was simply funny.

'I don't think she'd do that.'

'I wouldn't put it past her.'

Oh God, thought Charlet, I wish I could feel strongly about something.

'I think perhaps I shouldn't see you for a bit. Just till she's quietened down,' he said.

Charlet knew what he'd been up to.

'You made love to her last night. After you'd slept with me, you went home and stuck it in her, it's disgusting slushing around in–people like that,' she felt like saying, the personal affront jogging her into something sharper than her usual laissez-faire morality.

'You don't mean that,' she said aloud, not as a protest, more as a statement of fact.

'You're quite right,' he said. 'I don't.'

Suddenly she was tired.

She left the Waiting Room early that evening. She had let him make love to her because she needed the reassurance of physical sensation, and it seemed a pity to waste the pretty panties, but once was enough. Jamie sulked because he liked to spin things out, and she'd said she had to get home. But they had a drink, kissed, and separated cheerfully enough. It was Friday, the rump end of the week, James's least favourite day.

'It's like New Year's Eve in miniature,' he said, 'a hebdomadal bag of filth.'

She had heard him say it before, so some of the pungency was missing, but she had liked him for his long words and she smiled complaisantly as he drove off to spend the weekend sticking it in his demanding wife. He seemed to have a penchant for dominant women. Bunny, whoever she was, didn't sound dominant, but even rabbits had teeth and claws.

As she retrieved her car from the Company garage, she suddenly remembered she'd meant to tell him she didn't want to see him any more.

Maybe it's just as well, she reflected, it might be clever to keep him on until something better turns up.

She realized it wasn't exactly the nice thing to do, but she felt vulnerable with the weekend in front of her. Nice people do nasty things, she thought. That's the difference between literature and life.

9

But was she nice?

Her mother had always taught her that nice was a terrible thing to say or be. And yet, it seemed to her, you had to carry around with you the idea that you liked yourself. There were certain things you did and certain things you didn't. It just depended what they were, that was all. You used people if they were using you, or if you couldn't help it, or if it seemed they wanted to be used. It was the same with her. People used her. Men used her when they looked at her in meetings with see-through eyes. The whole of Nature seemed to be like one of those impenetrable country dances where sooner or later everyone gets twirled.

As she guided the little sports car up through the labyrinth of the carpark and out into the underpasses and ring roads that led home, she found herself thinking about her mother again.

It was a subject that kept floating up in her mind at the most unexpected times, with irregular regularity, like bubbles in a home-made winemaker's demijohn.

Her very name was her mother's choice. On some expedition connected with the school – her mother had been a teacher – she had found it on a gravestone in some out of the way churchyard, looked it up when she got home, and found it was the spelling in common use in the seventeenth century, the English version of Charlotte. Mother was always unearthing things like that.

Not that Charlet minded her name. Quite the reverse, it was a talking point, not so strange that you felt embarrassed nor so common that it didn't declare her to be a little special.

The other thing her mother had given her, apart from features that were sharply good-looking and 'good, long walking legs', her mother's phrase, was a determination not to be 'a woman in a man's world', another favourite reiteration.

Actually, Charlet would not have minded settling for being just that, since her nature included a generous dollop of some ancestor's idleness, but Charlet had had resistance thrust upon her at an early age – which, together with an admixture of her mother's stubbornness, made her adhere to at least notional acceptance of the rule. She could make the world her own, her mother said, and it seemed like a perfectly sensible idea. History and the male crisis of confidence were behind her.

Her father had been a soldier, but Charlet was the only evidence that he had ever shared a home with her mother.

'The only thing you could say about him was that he was marginally more human than an inseminator syringe,' her mother used to say when asked why she married him.

They had been divorced years ago.

Charlet remembered him bouncing her on his knee.

'This is the way the soldier rides . . .'

She had fallen off a little garden wall and had cried.

'Courage,' he had told her, 'you're in the front line now.'

Later, her mother said, he had died in a small war.

Charlet had not taken her mother's teaching entirely on trust. Indeed, she had gone through a rebellious stage in her teens when, finding that she was pretty, she discovered that she could have the world much as she wanted it.

At length, having no particular talent for teaching or chemistry or engineering or medicine or sport – all of which pursuits would have met with her mother's approbation – she ended up by doing a secretarial course at the local college, and there she met Howard, an art student with a talent for funny drawings. At this point, they became friends rather than lovers.

After a couple of years in an apartment in town, during which time she occasionally saw him but had affairs with other boys, she suddenly decided that she'd had enough of this patchy sort of existence, and that she should marry Howard. She described it to herself, though not to Howard, as getting marriage over.

Her mother still had all sorts of plans for her. She had reconciled herself to her daughter's lack of aptitude in any one obvious direction, but she was undoubtedly bright, and with a secretarial diploma one could get a toe on the ladder of television, journalism, social services, local government, even marketing. But, with the announcement of her engagement, all these hopes were now dashed.

'It'll kill me if you do this,' said her mother.

'Mother, I've got my own life to lead.'

'Life? You call it life? Diapers and detergents? Kitchen sinks and hot stoves? Your intellectual horizons bounded by the supermarket and the washeteria?'

'Things have changed, mother. It isn't like that now. There's disposable nappies and washing machines.'

'You'll see. You'll see.'

'Anyway, Howard and I are in love.'

It wasn't true. She had never discovered in herself the real preparedness to be hurt which goes with the emotion. But she knew her mother would rise to the remark.

'Love?' her mother reiterated, rolling her eyes and snorting like a charger modelling for an equestrian statue, 'Love? Love was invented by the troubadours to cuckold the absent crusaders. The ancients regarded it as a disease. Love? Love is simply sublimated secretion.'

Older people didn't seem to realize that you had to build experience for yourself. Other people's experience was like other people's toothache. You knew they had it but somehow it didn't impinge.

Anyhow, they married and it didn't kill her mother. To support Howard and herself, while he was finishing his course, she took a job as secretary at Butterby's, and from this she graduated to Personal Assistant to the Marketing Director, to Assistant Brand Manager, this advance to some extent mollifying her mother and allaying her worst fears.

Then she left to have a family.

The arrival of children, which would have transported most grandparents into raptures of benignity, seemed actually to finish her mother off. Her sad life and rigorous self-discipline had perhaps weakened her constitution, but the shock of seeing her daughter become the parent of a male sent her into a depressive decline from which she never emerged. She died a few months later in an agnostic convent.

Quite soon, however, perhaps because her mother was no longer around to be resisted, Charlet found herself beginning to come round to her views.

She started to resent the amount of time she was required to spend on other people. One baby was exhausting, two were three times as exhausting. Her parents had never spent this time on her. She knew she should feel an instinctive love and tenderness for them but somehow, as with her inability to be in love, she sensed in herself a distance, even a disinterest in the small creatures. She knew it wasn't natural, that it had nothing to do with feminism or philosophy, it was simply an unfortunate quirk that actually made her something of a freak. But freaks can't reason themselves out of their freakishness. There was a small part of her life that she felt wasn't nourished and, as is the paradoxical way with such things, it grew and grew.

Ostensibly, her life with Howard and their children, Natasha and Paul, settled into the customary routine of young married life.

Howard had taken a job as an art director at an advertising agency (even though his preference was for cartoons) to maintain family income while she was out of action. But he wasn't a company man, offices dried him up, he said. And because he didn't like it, he was unsuccessful and poor value when he got home.

It was at this point she started to keep in regular touch with some of the people at Butterby's. It was inevitable that she should sooner or later go back there. (As it happened, it was sooner – just as soon as Natasha was three and old enough to go to nursery school.)

Perhaps because she was a freak, she didn't have many friends in the neighbourhood. Other wives soon realized she was not a candidate for baby talk and coffee mornings, but she did have a friend called Martha who lived a couple of doors away. While the children toddled in the garden, Martha would regale her with hash shortbread and a fund of wonderful smutty stories.

'Did you hear the one about the newly opened sperm bank for geniuses?'

'You're about to tell me.'

'Their first customer was this very old Nobel Prize winner. The nurse looked a bit doubtful because he seemed so old and frail, but he was very determined. So she sent him along to the room with his bottle, and waited for him to come back. Five minutes. Ten minutes. Twenty minutes. She started to get anxious and sent for the Matron. They gave it another five minutes, and then they dashed along and burst open the door. The old man was sitting on the bed very red in the face, and they rushed up to him with saline drips at the ready. "Oh there you are," he said. "Glad you came along. Thing is, I just can't make it out. I've tried with my left hand. I've tried with my right hand. I've tried with both hands. And I still can't get the top off the bottle."'

At other times, they would make up absurd fantasies about their neighbours.

'The Thorntons,' Martha would say, 'tell me about the Thorntons.'

The Thorntons were a smug and primly prosperous couple who lived just down the road and were always complaining about other people's dogs or children playing outside their front gate.

'The Thorntons,' Charlet told her, 'do not mate like

ordinary mortals. They have no reproductive bits. Under-neath they're like teddy bears. They had a little operation to smooth them off. They are similarly nipple-less. And their navels have been grouted and made good. They excrete once a week in small ready-tied bio-degradable grow-bags.'

'Do they ever have sex?'

'Not through normal channels. Occasionally they eat gooseberry jam on small slices of Lithuanian sausage to the music of Rimsky-Korsakov rendered on a Wurlitzer organ by a one-armed Nubian.'

'This is their sex?'

'Certainly.'

'Do they . . . you know . . . have orgasms?'

'No.'

'They must have something. Surely something must happen.'

Charlet thought about it. Suddenly her brow cleared.

'They don't have orgasms,' she said, definitively. 'They have organasms.'

They never passed the Thorntons' house after that without saying 'Wurlitzers', and giggling stupidly.

She'd told Howard about their stories, thinking he'd like a joke, but he'd been quite stuffy about it.

'We have to live with the neighbours,' he'd said. 'It doesn't do to get their backs up.'

'But it's only a joke.'

'Jokes are serious,' he said, 'you discover that when you spend your life thinking about them.'

'Like Snackerjacks.'

They had heard endlessly about the new product being developed as a result of the Fastfoods takeover.

'Very much like Snackerjacks. Jokes and Snackerjacks have much in common. Light but unguessable in origin. The stuff that dreams are made of.'

He was so quiet and patient, even when he disagreed

47

with her profoundly, that now driving back down the familiar avenues, she felt quite guilty about her affairs. But she knew that if she didn't have them, she'd start to feel shut in; that life was over; that the rewards weren't worth the effort; and she might have to leave for good, which she didn't want, not yet, not till something really definite came up.

Life, she thought, was an undignified tug of war between ambition and insecurity.

10

Parking the car on the slithery gravel which he spent hours raking while he thought of jokes, she felt a little surge of affection for them as she glimpsed them all sitting together in the kitchen, no doubt planning the gastronomic miracle for Sunday lunch.

She sometimes felt like this on Fridays. She would return, fretted by the week, almost able to convince herself that she could sink back into the undemanding nickety nackety of married housewifedom.

It was helped, of course, by the fact that Howard ran the house so well there was almost nothing arduous for her to do, but there would be clothes to buy, shops to browse through, crockery to replace, wine to buy, little snippings and trowellings to be undertaken in the garden.

Much of the time she would spend with her feet up, catching up on magazines. Or there would be a dinner party on Saturday night to help get ready; she'd lay the table with Howard, consult with him about the wine. Wine was her province. She had come to know a certain amount about it through eating out so much at work.

Other times, she'd slip round the corner and spend

hours chatting with Martha, while her husband Trevor played golf.

Sometimes she would escort the children to parties or the cinema, though they really preferred Howard to take them. She didn't mind their preference. It would have been awkward had it not been so.

Very occasionally, she and Howard would make love on Saturday night. He would pounce upon her carefully as if she were a joke he was trying to get right.

By the end of the weekend, she'd be half ready to settle for the comfortable dispensations of domesticity, to give up the office and to devote herself to family life – and half eager to be away again in the cut and puff of Fastfoods and the just-a-little-dangerous dance of dalliance that was her due as the Company's most sought-after up-and-comer.

She was treading a rope, she knew; the two halves of her life were ultimately irreconcilable; but the rope did seem reasonably broad and soft. If she didn't look down too much, it seemed to be getting her where she wanted to be, which was nowhere in particular, but travelling.

'Hullo all,' she said as she marched into the kitchen, misty with delectable aromas.

'Hullo, Group Brand Mummager,' they cried. 'We've saved a capital treat for you. It's in the oven.'

They had fallen into the habit of using words like capital after reading through some of the piles of old magazines which Howard collected for possible joke leads.

'Capital, is it?' she smiled.

'More like top-hole.'

How sweet of them, she thought. What was she doing in that ridiculous job when she could be here, lapped in smells of fresh ironing and cinnamon cakes. She smiled at them and opened the oven door.

A monster like a cross between a slavering dog and a sea serpent sprang out, turning her knees to junket.

'Wha . . . What? . . .' was all she could say.

'It's only a poor old behemoth,' said her son.

'A . . . what?'

She had clutched at a chair, and now slumped into it. Everyone was laughing. They didn't seem to see her discomfiture. She tried to pull herself together. You're in the front line now.

'A behemoth for Daddy's new monster range.'

'I had to make a model to see how it'd work in an envelope,' her husband said. 'You open the envelope and it springs out like a jack in the box. It's the latest thing, paper engineering, you know. The Japs have been making great strides.'

'But they haven't got a beeheemoth,' shrieked her daughter delightedly.

'No,' agreed her father, seriously. 'I think we're on to something big.'

'That's a joke,' explained her son. 'Behemoth is an enormous creature in Hebrew.'

Charlet had by now managed to regain her composure. The trouble was with these jokes, you couldn't lose your temper because you risked being branded a spoilsport. It was only a joke, after all, wasn't it?

'Don't ever do that again,' she burst out, disregarding her better judgement, and losing her temper.

'The effect is somewhat diminished by repetition,' observed her husband, mildly, 'which is one of the main drawbacks to the idea.'

'Spoilsport,' said her children in unison, 'can't take a joke, spoilsport.'

'I've had a hard week,' she began. 'I don't expect to come home to a madhouse. I see little enough of you as it is.'

'Whose fault is that?' said her daughter in husbandly manner.

'Natasha . . .' said her father reprovingly.

Now Charlet was really wound up.

'If you like to make the money,' she shouted at him, 'I'll stay at home and play silly buggers with bits of paper. As you don't seem capable of supporting us, perhaps you'd refrain from getting up my nose when I do get back. You might think I'd earned myself a bit of peace.'

She knew this was not only unfair but bad diplomacy. The children shot furious glances at her. Her daughter burst into tears.

'Why d'you always come home and spoil everything?' she asked.

'Natasha . . .' her father repeated.

Charlet stalked furiously across and opened the kitchen door.

'It was only a poor old behemoth-in-a-box,' said her husband.

Charlet slammed the door and went upstairs to call Poppy, conscious she'd made a fool of herself.

'I hate Mummy,' she heard her daughter say.

She was just aware of a tiny imp, lurking behind the gorse bushes of her mind, who seemed to be asking whether her husband, in spite of his mild manner and careful husbandry, might not actually have maliciously set the whole thing up. She dismissed the notion immediately. There was nothing sinister about Howard. It'd be like going out for a walk and coming back to find your familiar house a deserted shell.

11

Luddington the Liftman was generally considered to be slightly nuts.

Nothing serious of course, but all the same eccentric. It was rumoured he believed himself to be the hereditary servant of the Celtic god Lud, Lord of the Great Abyss.

In other respects, he was an admirable Liftman. And his obsession with his office made him admirably confidential. People did not have to stop their conversations in front of Luddington, knowing that he had his mind on other matters.

He very rarely spoke of his calling, and certainly not to any but a few highly favoured long-time employees, usually in the Packaging and Despatch Department.

So it was with a mixture of astonishment tinged with flatteredness that Charlet heard him address her on the way up to her room on Monday morning.

'You know Lud, of course,' he remarked.

She looked at him in surprise. She had heard of his foible, but had previously exchanged no more than a ritual 'Good morning' with him.

He was a small man with a large droll head upon which his peaked hat clung like a tree-frog.

'I'm afraid I don't, Luddy,' she replied.

'Lud knows you,' he remarked cryptically. 'This very building is built on his temple. Lud don't like that. Lud groans. Hear these lifts?'

'Who is Lud?' she asked, although someone or other had told her.

'He's like Pan. You know what they said? Great Pan is dead. But they never said Great Lud is dead.'

The lift arrived at her floor.

Luddington supervised the automatic door with a flourish.

'His symbol is the yawning chasm,' he said, and then, 'have a nice day.'

It would be a good story to tell at the next Executives' Lunch; and somehow it proved a good omen.

Things did indeed seem to get better. She managed to finish her report – she had worked on it over the weekend while the family visited a Craft Centre – and the odious Foxworth didn't demand dinner with her as he'd suggested last week. Instead, he proposed lunch.

'I don't know. When?'

'Today?'

'I'm afraid I'm busy today.'

'Couldn't you get out of it? Who is it? Some randy adman? Make the bugger sweat.'

'Well! . . . maybe. All right.'

As it happened, it turned out to be not such an ordeal after all. He wasn't so full of himself with just one person around. She always found it intriguing, slightly exciting, when somebody could be so different. You didn't know where you were with them. Most people were so predictable.

He talked intelligently about his plans for his various brands, about his divorce, his flat, his enthusiasm for sailing, and only over coffee did he put a hand on her knee. Sex was clearly one of his other little hobbies. She moved slightly in order to pick up her bag for a cigarette, and he had to let go. Rather to her surprise, he didn't try again.

'You know,' he said, 'you're an extraordinary person.'

'Oh? How so? I think I'm pretty normal.'

He snorted over his cigar.

'My God,' he said, 'you've got away with a lot in your

53

life. Has no one ever challenged some of the things you say?'

'I don't know what you mean.'

'You know damn well what I mean. You're like a sort of canny tennis player. It's not that your strokes are wonderful. You just let us make all the mistakes.'

'Is that why you think I'm surprising?'

'Partly. You seem somehow detached.'

'Not from the job, I'm not.'

Was this where the third degree started, she wondered.

'No, not from the job. From the world. You don't seem one of us.'

'Oh, I don't know. Maybe that's the way I look.'

'Oh on the contrary, you look very much like part of the world. The very curve of your neck, there, just under your ear, invites the most terrestrial imaginings.'

'The way people look,' she wanted to say, 'is often the opposite of the way they are.'

She wisely kept it back, watching him warily as she lit another cigarette.

He was perhaps not much more than medium height, a couple of inches under six-foot, but his spare figure, cropped iron-grey hair, iron-grey moustache, and gold-rimmed glasses lent an impression of stature as much cerebral as physical. His eyes were perhaps a little too close together, and maybe a mite on the small side, but they were very bright and glittery. They always seemed to be looking through or ahead to something that wasn't entirely apparent to the groundlings.

Was she a groundling? She decided she was not. She knew what he was looking forward to.

She continued to take stock of him. The movements, precise. The voice deep and resonant if a little harsh, the ears stuck out a little, and with small wisps like cloudlets sprouting out of each cave, as if a sybil lurked within.

Normally she would have said he was neither particularly attractive nor the reverse. But there was power in the expression, authority in the glittery eye, something even of threat in the manner that made him on closer inspection both alarming and attractive. He was a snake charmer, she decided. He'd play his little tune and you'd do what he liked – that is, if you were a snake.

She shook herself inwardly; what sort of talk was this? Was he going to recommend her for Group Marketing Manager or was he not? She supposed she should play along with him, though Poppy would say this was mere sexism.

'My friend Poppy would say you were a sexist,' she said, sipping the last of her wine.

'A revolting word. What is this drowsy Poppy?'

'She is Advertising Manager for a small trade journal.'

'I daresay she is plain. That's why she tries to dress up her physical disadvantage with sociological cant.'

'Sexism again.'

'Not at all. Those who are plain are naturally envious of a talent they do not possess. That is, if they are ambitious. If they were honest they would go the whole hog and propose a Beauty Tax.'

'What have looks to do with a career in marketing, or advertising, or anything, apart from the obvious?'

'A very great deal. Men use sex in their careers – not usually in the same way as women, but sex nonetheless. It is a power, a drive, a confidence. It is a quality that other men find impressive, and women find . . . sexy. A woman uses her sex in another way, that's all. She is desirable, good to look at, men want to please her, to stroke . . . to touch . . .'

'Yes, but . . .'

'It's when women get the idea that the way to equitable advancement is to behave like a man . . . to strut and furrow the brow and stride and loud-mouth everyone . . . it's then, that's sexism if you like.'

'Poppy doesn't strut. Though she does have a slight moustache.'

She felt a momentary pang of disloyalty, but he didn't know Poppy did he?

'There you are, then,' he said, waving for the bill, 'but you, you're not like that. In spite of being more feminine than most – in your appearance, your instinctual capacity – you seem at the same time to display a rare masculinity in your intellectual processes too.'

It was when people started talking about her intellectual processes that she knew they wanted to sleep with her. However, if people weren't flattered by flattery, flattery would go out of fashion.

'Oh?' she smiled, pleased in spite of her intellectual processes.

'As I say, you're detached. Cutting out all that liberated cant, I'd say that was a masculine quality. "Cast a cold eye on life, on death" and all that. Anyway, it's an admirable trait in a businesswoman. We value the ability to take an overview,' he mimicked the management cliché.

Detached? Perhaps. The truth was, she supposed, she'd never really felt that she belonged anywhere. It had always been rather an advantage. She was a sort of stationary passer-by around whom the real people went about their business. But because she was still and they were bustling, she was sometimes able to see more clearly what went on.

She gave herself a little shake. It was clever of him to have latched on to her tendency to self-dramatize.

She looked at him again, glad she was not a snake.

'Do I get Nut Puffs?' she asked.

She knew Larry wanted it; but, what the hell, he had after all spoken of leaving.

'How d'you know about Nut Puffs?' he asked, and then, to her surprise: 'If you'll have dinner with me next week, I'll think about it.'

She suddenly found that her earlier aversion to the man had almost entirely evaporated. True, there was a little self-preserving corner of her mind that continued to have its reservations, but it certainly wasn't enough to risk losing Fastfoods' brightest baby.

It was when they were walking back to the office after lunch that it happened again. They had taken the longer way round, skirting a wide stretch of derelict ground that had been cleared of rubble and was awaiting redevelopment. Inside, weeds undeterred by marketing concepts fizzed against the wire fence and creepers frolicked at the faded notice that warned of Guard Dogs. Whether it was the sight of so much Nature in undress, the sudden reminder among the seasonless lawnlets of the city, the tubs and terraces, of the unstoppable thrust of disorderly things in the ground, or the potency of the Barolo, or the trickle of guilt about betraying not one but two friends over lunch, but suddenly she experienced again the tremendous feeling of pressure that she'd felt in the road at home the other night. All Creation's seeds seemed to be bursting and budding in her head.

She turned to the appalling Bruce who wasn't so appalling after all, but he was gazing up at a couple of white-overalled men in one of those swinging cradles who were cleaning the windows on the fourth floor of the soaring new chrome-and-glass block that had risen on a previous patch of convolvulus and ground-elder.

As she looked up with him, she had once more that strange sensation. She thought, if I stop holding them, the rope will snap, the men will fall.

And once again she turned away, knowing it was ridiculous, until suddenly she heard Bruce exclaim: 'Oh my God.'

She didn't dare look up but waited numbly for the high-pitched screams and the terrible thump as the bodies hit the ground.

Then Bruce said: 'I've made a booboo. I've just remembered I arranged a meeting in my office for quarter of an hour ago. I'd better run. See you later.'

She looked up, and the two men swung blithely on the building's side as they had before. There was nothing wrong with their rope, although the same couldn't be said for their manners.

'Oi, oi, show us your legs, darling.'

She turned and walked slowly back to the office.

12

It was strange how your perceptions altered once you were inside the building again.

Through the tinted windows, beyond the air-conditioning, out of sound of the breathing lifts, the vast sprawl of the city spread out like a wall map, giving the impression that the real world was false, and that only the office had three-dimensional substance.

Outside, you could have the feeling that you were wandering about in some vast open-plan film-set. But walking through the secretaries' pen on the fourteenth floor or past the busy hum of the Research Interview Hall on the ninth, you could sense the true pulse and tremble of reality.

For many of the denizens of John Keats House, this dense little Company world was the powerful centre of their dreams and aspirations. It made them choose Company cars, without consulting each other, all of the same colour (metallic blue this year).

It made them say, with a self-pleasing mock-deprecating little chuckle: 'Do you know, I think I really *am* a Fastfoods person.'

For indeed, there were only two things to be. You were either a Fastfoods person, or you were not – in which case it was wiser to leave with all speed, or you'd feel each day that passed squeezing the colour out of you until you too were finally drawn, still flapping and struggling, into that strange domain of anti-matter, bizarre dimensions, and slow-time. (The result was almost exclusively bad for Fastfoods, since the brighter executives tended not to be Company people. Decision makers of the real sort rather than the Affleck variety, intuitive entrepreneurs, perceptive creators, all found the atmosphere too thin, the goalposts too unguessable, the ball too heavy. It was one of the reasons why Fastfoods had slowed down in every area except Company politics in the last few years.)

But Charlet, with that instinctive sense of positioning that had served her so well in product development, had found a third option.

She hovered in the singularity between outside and in, belonging to neither one reality nor the other. The posture, it was true, was rather more use to her at Fastfoods than it was in the outside world, so she addressed herself a whisker more to the Company rather than the home face. But independence was the thing.

The danger was, she sensed, that some quite minor irregularity, some trepidation beyond her control could upset the equilibrium. Only while she maintained her outsideness would she be inviolable.

But then, if she didn't worry about it, all would be well. It had always been one of her guiding principles, and it had worked admirably so far.

The telephone on her desk rang all afternoon. She felt a little sleepy from her lunch. Her in-tray was full of small pressing pointless pieces of paperwork. Annoyance built upon irritation without subduing her sense of inertia.

This was the sort of time she would normally slip into a hyper-drive of detachment away from the dangers of heavy density, but this time there seemed to be one or two wobblies in the mechanism.

13

Someone had said to her once, a jettisoned swain (could it have been Larry?), 'I feel sorry for you, Charlet.'

She had paused, pulling on her panties, one of those last acts of careless intimacy, her naked breasts unloving and interrogative.

'Sorry, how come?'

'You're emotionally undernourished. It's not that you can't feel, it's just that you don't know how to. That mother of yours has a lot to answer for.'

'You may be right,' she said, aware that there was some truth in the accusation, 'but what do you suggest I do about it? Anyway, is it so wrong? Love seems to cause people more trouble than it's worth. Like eating crayfish. Infinite pains to reach very little meat.'

'You can't experience pleasure without knowing about pain.'

'That's like saying you can't have sugar without medicine.'

'Love's different.'

'Love is physical. Like food. That's the way I thought you men were supposed to like it. You can enjoy a meal without falling in love with it.'

'As I said, I feel sorry for you.'

She found herself echoing her mother's words.

'Love is simply an invention of the Middle Ages to help them distinguish between a fuck and a rape.'

The conversation came back to her (the incident of the window-cleaners, the heaviness of the afternoon, had induced a mood of introspection) as she drove down to see Poppy that evening.

This time it was a genuine assignation – she still played the game of providing excuses for her absences from home. Once that was gone, you might as well pack up and live separately.

Poppy lived in an area of town that had experienced various tides of fashion.

Big red-brick houses, predominated, built halfway through the previous century as prosperous merchants moved west along the river; then vacated as the Underground made distant pastures more appealing; and next taken over by artisan families who had never really cared for them. So they had declined like old court favourites, starved of attention and benefit, superseded by younger rivals, showing their age the more they came down in the world, at length shared out like common harlots; patched, cracked and raddled, teetering on the edge of disintegration . . . and then, at the last minute, miraculously reclaimed as the district started to rise again.

People no longer wanted to spend two or three hours every day travelling to their place of work, and the locality was suddenly taken up by the more perspicacious estate agents.

The houses now basked in an Indian summer of second youth. True, not all of them by any means had been restored to single-family residences, but the old gimcrack divisions had been replaced by elegant walls of brick and timber designed by fashionable young architects, and whereas a score of years before you might have found twenty people living in a villa's four storeys, today you would be hard put to it to find more than one person to a floor. Most of the leaseholders were young executives and expensive secretaries who, whether for reasons of love or business, were not even there half the time.

It was a trim, prosperous, neatly ordered, half-inhabited sort of neighbourhood with just that whiff of panic about it that distinguishes places that have seen hard times.

Charlet had known Poppy since they were children. Their mothers had been as near to friends as Charlet's mother ever got.

They had attended the same schools. Often they would stay with each other in the vacations, or go on adventure holidays together, the classic combination of pretty girl and plainer best friend.

When they finally left school, they both attended the same secretarial course, Poppy passing out nearly top of the class and Charlet getting the best job; but Poppy always revelled in her friend's success. Charlet knew she was too caring to be jealous. They settled in to a small apartment together in what was then an unfashionable suburb.

Perhaps because of other qualities beyond her looks (though certainly not impeded by these), Charlet had always been the more outgoing of the two. More self-assured, she believed that if you didn't think about bad things, they wouldn't happen.

Poppy, on the other hand, was a worrier, which was perhaps why she was accident-prone, or was it the other way round?

In appearance, she was a complete contrast to Charlet. Dark and frizzy-haired, inclined to plumpness, she found men on the whole disappointing (naturally she got on well with Charlet's mother), always fancying the unattainable. Taken for a ride by married men, let down by one-night stands, her weight was a constant problem. She only had to eat a bun to swell up like a puff ball. So she alternately fasted to the point of debility and then, when made miserable by one of her ill-suited cavaliers, she would embark on terrible passionate binges of chocolate and gingernuts.

As Charlet rose through the ranks of secretary and Personal Assistant, Poppy was left behind, tied to her typewriter and a series of tyrannical bosses. But Charlet, though her horizons widened, never abandoned her completely. There was part of her that depended on Poppy.

A temporary break came when she moved out of the flat to stay with her first serious lover, a junior television executive, but when that faded out there was always her old room there in the flat, smelling of gas-leak and hair conditioner.

The pattern was repeated several times. Then suddenly, after almost two years, Charlet announced she was going to get married.

At this, Poppy became considerably upset. She was, of course, overjoyed for her friend, but to some extent she had depended on her to bring the world, as it were, to her door.

It was true, while Charlet had been away, Poppy had entertained a retinue of sorts but it had been dubious and intermittent. She had had an abortion at one juncture (which Charlet had completely missed, being on holiday in Malaysia at the time). Later Poppy had contracted both clap and herpes – not, it had to be said, at the same time but in unseemly succession. All this had been safely weathered because Poppy knew that Charlet would in the end return and everything would be as it always had been. But the idea of her marriage finally rubbed some of the adhesiveness from the relationship.

Finally making the ranks of executive, Poppy had applied for a job in one of her PR company's offices in Australia – and, apart from a postcard or two, the girls had hardly seen each other for five years. Charlet missed her undemanding support but never wrote to say so.

When Poppy returned, Charlet hardly recognized her. Having always been plump, Poppy was now thin and leathery. What had they done to her in Sidney? Bisexual beach boys? Lizard-eyed lesbians? Poppy had become a pachyderm.

She'd leased out the apartment when she'd been away, but now came back to take it on again, pleased to find the area had gone up in the world. She had even arranged to buy the lease, so she was now a woman of property; something you could never imagine of the old Poppy.

But of course nothing had really changed underneath, and a couple of evenings together had them both back to their old easy exchange.

After a year, their relationship was almost as close as ever. There was still the strangeness of having a scrawny best friend – which she now discovered was all down to some pills (Charlet had actually preferred her plump but didn't like to say so), – and a harder edge in her attitude to life, men especially, which was doubtless all to the good.

Poppy had worked up an enthusiasm for what she called the modern visual arts, meaning film and television, since her return. One of the accounts she handled at her (now) advertising agency was a television station, and she'd thrown herself into the business enthusiastically. Poppy liked to be committed.

All those visits to the cinema weren't totally fictitious, thought Charlet as she turned, with a pretty change of gears, down the leaf-strewn chestnut avenue leading to the flat. All in all, the new Poppy was probably an improvement on the old, but just a little bit of her said it would like to have kept the old disaster zone.

Howard found Poppy something of a bore, but the bond between girlfriends is something men seldom understand.

'She's so intense,' he'd say. 'She used to be a bumble-bee and now she's a leatherjacket.'

Howard could have an incisive turn of phrase which he'd normally only unleash on his joke cards.

Charlet didn't argue. She valued Poppy too much as an excuse for many of her little excursions to want to try and persuade Howard out of his antipathy.

'I'm so glad you're late,' said Poppy as Charlet sat down in one of the fashionable wicker armchairs that had sprung up around the flat. 'I've just got back from a drink with Steve.'

Charlet was often late. An Aquarian, she had read somewhere, has her mind on higher things than punctuality. She doubted that Poppy had only just returned. It was one of Poppy's old tricks, unnecessarily making her feel at ease.

'I thought I'd warned you about Steve,' she said. 'It's a name I invariably associate with trouble.'

'I associate most men's names with trouble,' said Poppy, 'and I'm usually right. Drink? There's Valpolicella or Valpolicella.'

Poppy busied herself with pouring from the already half-empty bottle. She seemed just a little drunk. It was a quality that various of her friends seemed to be having in common these days. Charlet hoped she wouldn't start telling her about her sex life.

'Now,' said Poppy, handing over the glass and sitting down schoolgirlishly, 'tell me all about it. The dirt. Everything.'

'Hmhm,' she shook her head, 'you first. How about this Steve?'

Steve was the married man she was currently seeing.

'We had a row last week. He doesn't like his wife but he loves his children.'

'So what's new?'

'I told him I wouldn't see him again.'

'And?'

'I saw him last night. We had a fabulous time.'

'That's about par for the course. What next?'

'I don't know. Muddle on. Where have all the unmarried men gone?'

'The one I had lunch with today's unmarried, well, divorced. I work with him. He's quite a toad. Trouble is, attractive. Could be a bully. Never know where you are. You know? Chauvinist.'

'Sounds yummy.'

Charlet didn't tell her what Bruce had said at lunch, nor indeed did she repeat her own little piece of bitchiness.

'I shan't sleep with him,' she said.

'I wouldn't bet on it.'

'D'you know, I'm tired of all that. What I'd like . . . what I'd really like is a boyfriend, the way they were when we first went out. Just to have a laugh with, hold hands in the cinema, talk about things. You know?'

'You'd miss the bed bit.'

'I don't know. All that groping and self-doubt and smells. Do you know what the new Dictionary of Slang has as a synonym for Sexual Groping? I read it in the paper today.'

Poppy filled the glasses again.

'Not the foggiest.'

'"A handful of sprats."'

'That's disgusting.' Poppy wriggled enjoyably, then looked reflective. 'I never heard anyone say that,' she continued.

'It's bandied freely about the corridors of Fastfoods, I assure you,' said Charlet, 'especially after the office party. Sprats everywhere. Handfuls of 'em. The computer programmers especially.'

'You're joking,' exclaimed Poppy, delightedly. Then: 'Funny you should say that, we're having whitebait to start with.'

66

'I'm not sure I could eat them after that.'

But she did – and the steak and salad that followed. She noticed that Poppy was only toying with her food, though.

'Still not eating properly?'

'I'm allowed one meal every two days. Otherwise it's my diet. I couldn't go back to being fat again. You're so lucky, Charlet. You're able to eat anything. You're just lucky all round, let's face it.'

Charlet was surprised by this little outburst. She'd thought Poppy had got over all that.

'My marriage isn't exactly wonderful.'

'Yes, but you *are* married. The arrangement suits you.'

To Charlet's surprise, Poppy suddenly burst into tears. She sometimes did this, particularly when she was happy: but talk of marriage to Howard could hardly have occasioned an outburst of uncontainable rapture.

'What is it, Pops?'

'It's not my fault. I think we're losing the account.'

'The account?'

'PPTV. The television station. The one I handle.'

'Oh. Is that bad for you?'

'I didn't like to tell you earlier because I thought it'd spoil our evening.'

Oh dear. This was a regression.

'They won't sack you, though?'

'If there's nothing for me to work on, they will. Then I'll have nothing. No husband, no family, no job.'

'Well, never mind. You can come and work with us.'

She said it without thinking, a meaningless encouragement that she would have censored if she had believed Poppy would take her seriously. For some reason, she didn't want to share her working life with her friend. But Poppy was instantly elated.

'Really? You really mean it?'

'Yes . . . yes, I'm sure you can. I'll speak to someone

tomorrow. It may not be your kind of . . . place, though. You know. Big, impersonal, slow decisions, meetings, reviews . . .'

But Poppy didn't seem to hear.

'Oh Charlet, that's wonderful. I'd really like that.'

She gave her a big sniffly kiss on the doorstep, and stood there waving until Charlet was out of sight.

Really, Charlet thought, definitely regretting it now, I wonder if that's really quite such a good idea. One needs friends, yes. But wasn't Poppy perhaps a bit of a liability; could be used, maybe, against her in some way?

Never mind. It was late. Poppy was quite obviously over the top and rather pissed. She'd probably find the whole thing had been patched up in the morning. In fact, thought Charlet, as she accelerated across the flyover, and down the ring road, she was prepared to bet that it would be.

Was it her imagination, or was the limping figure on the walkway the tramp who had waved his arms at her the other day?

14

It had always been one of Larry's beliefs (according well with her own instincts) that one should have a secure grip either at work or home, never should lose one's hold on both at the same time. And though she was, of course, more than secure at the office, there had recently been these tremors, whether or not of her own making, that made her feel the need for a little home base-work.

So the next weekend she addressed herself to family life. The funny thing was, there was almost nothing for her to do. The shopping, the cooking, the cleaning all seemed to be taken care of. Her husband had his system perfectly worked out. His assistant, the mousy Pentelle, helped as much round the house during the week as she beavered in the drawing-office.

The children had now got to the age, nine and eight, when they had their own friends, and – when they weren't helping their father – seemed to spend much of the time at neighbours' houses.

So she found she had time to do some of the things she had put off until they had almost become written out of her consciousness. For instance, there was that pile of junk of her mother's that was sitting in the attic waiting to be sifted. And, since her mother had been cropping up in her thoughts recently, she decided to pull down the slidey aluminium stairs, and spend the afternoon having a sort-out.

It was when she was going through a box of old letters and papers that she came across a note from her father. She had always assumed he was dead since her mother had told her so, but now it seemed there was another possibility.

'Dear Joscelyn,' it read, 'I am sorry to hear that Charlet had such a bad asthma attack after I last saw her. Of course, if her health is at risk, I will do as you suggest and discontinue my visits. Indeed, if such is your wish, I will sever all connections with both you and her for I must confess I find being a fraction of a parent more upsetting than being none at all. As Bacon says, "he who hath a wife and family hath given hostages to fortune." It is perhaps fortunate that being in the Intelligence business I should so easily be able to divest myself of this professional inconvenience. Please tell Charlet at some appropriate moment that my absence from her life should not be taken as indifference. Yours, Edward.'

For some reason, this letter filled her with a quite unexpected feeling of pleasure. There had been a man who genuinely cared for her; and a man, it seemed, even from this short note, who was very different from the brutish warrior of her mother's description. She felt a surge of annoyance with her mother for using her mild childhood asthma as a weapon against him.

The next bundle of letters gave her more cause for contemplation. It included a short note from the Department informing Charlet's mother that her ex-husband was reported Missing. It did not say where or how. It did not say that he was dead.

An absurd thought grew in Charlet's mind, absurd because she had never consciously had any feeling of great loss about her father, accepting it as one of those physical accidents of life like the length of your nose that she should not have a male parent; but now it seemed to her possible that he might still be alive, held prisoner in some Iron Curtain Spandau; languishing, as her son would say, in durance vile. It seemed unlikely, indeed hardly credible; but the notion pleased her. She decided to do some research on it. There must be a record somewhere, someone who had known him, documents, a file. However impenetrable the Department, she was used to the innate obstructiveness of large organizations, and felt confident she could extract at least a hint of something to go on.

She came downstairs in a good mood, aware that she had to get ready for a local dinner party that evening.

Usually, after even a day's effort at trying to be domesticated, she would once more have the old feeling of running out of promise. It wasn't anything Howard or the children actually did. It was more a sense of closing down the shutters on a fertile and beckoning landscape, and turning instead inwards on to a desert which her family seemed to find perfectly congenial and life-sustaining.

Today, though, inspired by this faintest of ghosts of a

chance of a father still around somewhere, she came down in a good mood, wanting to tell them about it. But as she folded up the ladder, catching her neatly manicured finger in one of its runnels and breaking the nail, her momentary irritation was fuelled by the realization that the house seemed to be in uproar. Lights blazed in every room and horrified squeals and shrieks suggested some kind of nightmare visitation.

Suddenly both children raced around a corner as Howard, dressed in a grotesque outfit with two extra arms extending outwards from his waist, came crawling after them squirting at them with a sticky-web House of Nightmare ghoul spray.

'Sssss,' he said as they suddenly saw her, 'sssss. Here comes the Group Brand Mummager. She looks like a tasssty morsssssel.'

The children hooted with laughter as he squirted a great dollop of the stuff all over the hair she'd hoped she wasn't going to have to wash.

She tried to keep her sense of humour but she could feel the annoyance welling up in her like soda pop.

'Don't be cross, Mummager,' the children pranced around her, 'don't get in a wax, old bean.'

'Really,' she said to Howard, 'my hair. Look at it.'

'It's washable,' he said placatingly.

'She comes home after a hard week,' sang the children. 'All she wants is a little consideration.'

'Perhaps you ought to get ready,' suggested Howard. 'They're expecting us at 8.15. Pentelle's coming to baby-sit. We don't want to keep her waiting.'

His mention of the obsequious dreary Pentelle suddenly goaded her.

'Don't talk to me about keeping her waiting. What about wasting my time? I'm sick of hearing about Pentelle.'

'Now you know that's absurd. Pentelle is very good to us. She even does the ironing while she's babysitting.'

'And she reads stories,' said her daughter.

'And she sings us ditties,' said her son, 'she's a regular song-bird.'

'If you think Pentelle's so marvellous, why don't you marry her?' she enquired coldly to her husband.

'It's quite clear you don't need me,' chanted the children.

Who were these people?

'Now come along, children,' said Howard, 'leave your mother alone. Me too, come to think of it. Go and watch Mayhem Man. We've got to look pretty from the Makepeaces.'

She was still silent as they walked round the corner, half an hour later, to the Makepeaces' house in Buddleia Gardens.

It was not that she loved Howard or felt more than a general concern for the children, but something had been mooted that emphasized just how much her life depended on the idea of having them there. It secured her from further commitment while allowing her to circulate. The realization – now she came to consider it, it had been growing for some days – made her both alarmed and a little resentful. It was all right while she was on automatic pilot but it made her uncomfortable to be reminded too much of her balancing act.

She knew it was unfair and immature that she should feel about her family in that way, as mere counterpoises, but it didn't make it any better. Luckily, mild Howard had always seemed contented with the status quo. People told him how lucky he was to have such a talented, vivacious and beautiful wife. It seemed this was sufficient for him. And of course he needed the money she brought in.

But tonight, perhaps because of the thing about her

father, the tremors in the office, the premonition of accidents, the ragged figure with its outstretched arms on the ring road (and hadn't he been in the shopping precinct when she'd been ordering the Sancerre Rouge?), it all made her feel that the general glue she'd fixed about her life was coming just a little unstuck.

As if to confirm her inklings, the dinner party was a disaster.

The Makepeaces lived in an immaculate house in an immaculate road. Their dinners were always excellent: the food well presented, the wine judiciously chosen. Their guests would be either beautiful, interesting or successful, very often incorporating all these attributes in one person.

There would usually be a sprinkling of media people around. Bobby Makepeace worked as a TV producer on a current affairs programme.

These articulately informed people would flash their knowledge as readily as they would show their orthodontically corrected teeth – teeth that, if you were good-looking, you could unexpectedly find nibbling your ear – or, if you were vulnerable, you could suddenly discover lodged in your jugular.

This evening, there was a barrister present who was laying down the law: women, business, the profit motive, truth versus myth in the Bible, motor cars, wine, the Third World, terrorism, anti-matter, nougat; there seemed no branch of human activity or learning that his ravenous mind had not accommodated or would not regurge at you in quick little pellets of instant erudition.

Howard sat at the other end of the table making his pretty neighbours fall about with his repertoire of jokes and his pocketful of string.

The barrister, meanwhile, was spoiling for an argument, and spent the soup course deciding who best to have it with. He picked on Charlet as the most attractive woman in the room.

'Tell me,' he asked seeming serious, 'these ah these snack products of yours . . . are they any good?'

'Good?' she countered.

She had met people like him before.

'Are they ah nutritious . . . beneficial?'

'Not particularly.'

'Well, isn't that a little ah obscene?'

'I'm sorry?'

'In a world where people are starving, are ah dying like . . .'

He paused to avoid the cliché and to haul another gobbet of cornet de saumon fumé up to his mouth, where a morsel of it hung waggling as he articulated.

'No no,' he waggled, 'not like flies, that argues too much value . . . like bacilli . . . like germs . . . in some microbial disaster zone . . . that is the price we put on human suffering when we continue to make ah snacks which we ah market at a profit for our already overfed, indeed increasingly obese domestic population.'

Put in a less aggressive manner, Charlet might well have agreed with him, while perhaps suggesting that comparing developed with underdeveloped economies somehow does justice to the problems of neither. But it was clear that this was not the moment for good-natured give and take.

It was the self-satisfaction of the man that was so galling, she thought; as if the Law had anything to be proud of. And now, to her wrath, she heard the murmurs of approbation from others round the table – the wives who didn't work, the property men, the newsmongers, and even (could it have been?) her husband.

She held her tongue until the crème brulée arrived, and the barrister dug in with busy spoon. The talk had turned to racism and the underprivileged.

'You should know about definitions,' she announced to the barrister. 'Aren't privileges and rights rather different things? Don't privileges have to be earned? You should talk about the under-righted if you have to talk about them at all.'

She was good on definitions. Her mother had taught her to be.

The barrister paused with his spoon in mid-air. All eyes bent upon her. Suddenly she felt a little drunk, half reckless, half apprehensive.

Her husband made a deprecating noise.

'Charlet works for a consortium run on quasi-military lines. Only they don't fire cannonballs out of their guns but crispy-crunchy-snappy-tasty Snackerjacks,' and he did a ridiculous parody of the Snackerjack commercial.

There was a snigger from Bobby Makepeace, and the other women tittered maliciously. There was an expectant pause. This was the very stuff of a good dinner party.

'"They grin like a dog and run about the city,"' thought Charlet, recalling another favourite phrase of her mother's who, though a staunch atheist, had been brought up on the Bible. She had used it to warn her daughter against attractive-seeming men.

Charlet now opened her mouth to speak, and words for which she could not altogether feel responsible emerged.

'It always seems to me,' she said, addressing herself once more exclusively to the barrister, 'that people who wear philanthropic views on their sleeves often have the least charity in their hearts. But anyone with a scrap of sense can see what they're up to. They wear it all wrong. Like putting on a raincoat to stop yourself drowning.'

The barrister, though he clearly had something to say, could not resist another mouthful first. Then he opened his mouth to speak. Charlet dived in like a guillemot.

'Did no one ever tell you,' she enquired, 'not to talk

75

with your mouth full? That's a crème brulée not a witness you're demolishing, you know.'

No one had spoken like that to the barrister for longer than he could remember. In spite of her admonition, his mouth remained agape.

The other diners had a problem. Were they to rally round their man, albeit discomfited – and whoever was discomfited had to be a dodgy candidate for support – or were they to applaud the sally of the outsider? In the end they were paralysed by the necessity of making a decision and made none, applying themselves with neatly closing lips to the crust-clotted goo that would have nourished a whole family for a week in Upper Volta.

Charlet suddenly found a hand on her knee. Or it could have been the dog. Like everyone else in the Makepeace household it seemed sexually hyperactive.

After coffee, the sofa was moved aside, and some of the diners danced. Bobby Makepeace advanced and invited Charlet to join him on the floor. He danced very close, and she could feel his erection uncoiling inside his trousers like an indoor firework.

'Come down to the basement later,' he whispered thickly, 'I've got a blue video that'll make your bush stand on end.'

Suddenly the wine, the thudding of the music, her general feeling of disconnection, a touch of indigestion (crème brulée had never agreed with her), the sight of mild-mannered Howard rubbing his own indoor firework up the black silk-frocked thighs of the lawyer's girlfriend, all combined in a single sensation of bile. She had, ever since childhood, been noted for a tendency to queasiness in moments of tension.

She darted out into the hallway and through the passage to the back, past the kitchen where a large woman in a knacker's apron was doing the washing up amid mouthfuls of leftover, and out into the garden.

What was she doing with these people? Why could she not find where she wanted to be, or whoever it was she wanted to be with?

The night air soothed her like the Magdalen's ointment. A sickle moon flew over the housetops, spearing itself on the Makepeaces' television aerial. Somewhere in the distance, a star barked. A peace she had not known for years enfolded her. She shut her eyes. The very earth seemed to tremble through her, including her in its course, making her pursuit of whatever it was seem inconceivably minuscule, her whole life no more than a flicker on some cosmic particle scanner.

Just at that moment, a plump hand clamped itself across her left breast, wriggling like a squid for her nipple, while another lifted her dress – damn, she'd meant to come in a trouser suit against just such a contingency – and began scrabbling at her tights, somewhat impeded by a dog's exuberant tongue which kept trying, rather successfully, to get in on the action too.

'Get away, Trotsky, bugger off,' she heard Bobby Makepeace scold, and a squawk from the animal confirmed his displeasure, and then: 'God, you're sexy.'

Charlet kicked back hard, catching him on the shin and eliciting this time a human yelp.

That squares it for Trotsky, she thought

'You cow,' panted Bobby, 'what d'you go and do that for?'

'Tat for tit,' she said, and vomited, rather neatly, into a bird bath.

'Oh dear,' said Bobby, momentarily disconcerted.

'You people make me want to throw up,' she told him. She felt much better now. 'I'm going home. Tell Howard not to worry. I don't want to spoil the party.'

'But . . . but you can't do that. I'll get him.'

'No, really,' she said. 'Just ask him to bring my scarf when he comes. I'll go out by the side gate.'

And she walked down beside the house towards the road.

Bobby stood irresolutely where she had left him, half embarrassed, half glad to be rid of her. In the morning he'd have forgotten about it. It had all happened before. It would all happen again.

As she opened the gate, she could hear Trotsky greedily lapping at the bird bath.

There seemed to her something symptomatic in the sound.

15

She had started to have the dream again, a silly nightmare she'd had when she was four or five.

For a couple of years, she and her mother lived in a big house in the country with one of her father's aunts.

It was a difficult situation for her mother to be in, living in the house of one of her divorced husband's relatives. It was one of the reasons they eventually left. But at the time there was apparently no alternative.

Her mother went out to teach at a neighbouring school, and Charlet was left in the care of the old woman whose methods of child supervision were founded on two enlightened principles: they could do what they liked and go where they wanted.

'The only rule,' she would say, 'is No Trouble. Trouble's a nuisance. Can't stand Trouble. Keep out of Trouble, child.'

On the whole, Charlet had obeyed the instruction. Trouble, she had already discovered, seems to come when there's not enough room. And there was room and to spare at her great aunt's. There were large overgrown shrubberies and arbours: ruined balustrades and terraces, a kitchen garden full of mysterious sheds and locked doors in the wall, a rockery, a goldfish pool with a wickedly smiling boy pointing an arrow at you that dribbled water, a little paved box-hedge square with a sun dial; and as for the house itself, there were passages and landings, cellars and attics, and more floors than you'd think an old lady would know what to do with.

One night, Charlet dreamt that she'd been out playing in some distant part of the garden. But, as she returned, she began to feel a kind of general unease and dread. Something horrible was going to happen. Even the birds seemed to have gone. There was just one robin left, hopping on the sun dial, and he said to her quite kindly but sorrowfully: 'Look out, he's coming, you know.'

She hurried on with brick feet.

At last she came to the house with its steps and its big front door. She could feel whatever it was close behind her. She reached up and scrabbled at the front door and, just in time, it opened; she was safe.

But then the worst thing happened. As she looked round for her aunt, her mother, Annie the old cleaning-woman-cum-cook, she noticed that all the furniture in the hall had gone. With horrid dismay, she opened the dining-room door. No furniture. She tried the library. The shelves were bare of books.

All through the house she ran. There was no one to be found.

And now she knew that whatever was following her was in the house as well, following her up the stairs as she ran for her last chance, the top floor. But even as she raced along the corridor, flinging the doors wide, she knew that when she came to the end, there would still be nothing to save her. And so it was.

She opened the very last door with the thing panting and looming behind her and . . . and . . .

Typically, it was her great aunt who came to her bedside and soothed her.

'Gone?' she said, 'we haven't gone. Here I am, large as life and twice as ugly. Silly old Trouble. Course we haven't gone. Trouble's gone, not us.'

She was gone now.

Funny the old dream coming back again.

16

He collected her at the Waiting Room a few days later, where she gave him a glass of Kir Royale. She was wearing a rather dashing blue dress. He seemed impressed.

'Very nice,' he said appreciatively, sipping at the drink as if it were her mouth.

'Presumably you mean the Kir?'

She knew the question was arch, but he had that effect on her, almost as if he had set out to destroy the detachment upon which he had complimented her.

'You know perfectly well what I mean,' he said.

He took her to an intimate French restaurant on a hill overlooking the older part of the city. It was a residential area, and married couples sat around them, saying things they had said before to each other, disputing and disquisiting with quiet familiarity, over food they knew to be good because it was so expensive.

As a matter of fact, it was good as well. Charlet wasn't wild about French cooking, which had always seemed to her small, fiddly and over-dressed with certain surprise pieces like goose gizzard in your salad that suddenly seemed to negate all the artifice.

'Like putting a paper ruff on a rectum,' she said trenchantly to Poppy.

She didn't mind explaining this to Bruce because she knew he wasn't really paying for the meal, it was down to the Company, and therefore she had almost as much right to it as he did.

Also she wanted to show them both that she wasn't afraid of him.

He laughed.

Encouraged, she decided on another experimental line that she had censored before.

'There is a theory that the way people act is almost the exact opposite of what they are,' she said.

'And what is that supposed to mean?'

'Well. Like you for instance. You have a rather . . . brusque manner sometimes . . . even brutal I should think . . .'

'It goes with the name. Et tu, Bruce.'

He pronounced it in the Italian way with a hard c. It was clear he'd made the joke before. She decided it was time for her to make one too.

'You have a talent for hitting the snail on the head,' she said, and then pretending solicitude: 'You don't mind my saying this?'

'Not at all. I like to be called uncouth.'

She had the sudden feeling that perhaps she shouldn't have started this, it was like walking into a farmyard and suddenly finding a large barking dog. What to do now? Retreat, advance, or stand still?

'What I mean is, well, it's a compliment really.'

Nice Rover.

'Don't climb down,' he said ungraciously, 'spit it out.'

'Well, really, I suppose I mean that though you seem sometimes . . . brutal . . . you're really just trying to compensate for your intrinsic pleasantness.'

'What third-rate psychology for the liberated woman have we been reading?' he asked.

'There you go,' she said, 'that's what I mean.'

'Listen,' he said brutally, 'we men have given you women a whole lot of rope but you're not supposed to go flicking it at us.'

'What do we do with it, then?'

'Hang yourselves.'

She had walked in to that one.

'Nice Rover,' she said.

'What?'

She explained about the farmyard.

'You think I'm really nice at heart, and I'm a bit ashamed of it.'

'Could be.'

'What about some of the thugs of history? Hitler? Bluebeard? Nero?'

'I suppose the fact is,' she said, 'some people *are* the way they seem, and some people *pretend* to be the way they seem.'

'And which are you?'

She had an uncomfortable feeling he knew the answer to that.

'Ah,' she said, taking refuge in archness once more, 'that would be telling.'

'Coffee?' he asked, 'or shall we have it at your place?'

'Well, I er don't think . . .'

She didn't know what she thought.

'What's the matter, Charlet? You gone off me? Changing your psychology all of a sudden? You shouldn't be too mutable, you know. Look bad in your record.'

'My record?'

'This is an assessment dinner we've got ourselves here, Charlet. I'm doing the report in the morning.'

She didn't know whether he was serious or not. It was one of the things about him. He kept changing the tune.

'And another thing. Do you like having your nipples gently squeezed, or just a finger going round the outside?'

She was affronted. And yet she couldn't help laughing. There was something ridiculous about discussing her nipples in this dapper restaurant. She wished she could get rid of this feeling of panic.

'We'll take it at your place, hm?'

'Certainly not.'

But when they arrived, he walked in while she was saying goodbye.

'I didn't say you could come in.'

'Just a coffee, a brandy, and a screw?'

'No.'

'Not even a small one?'

'No.'

'Tiny watchmaker's size?'

'Absolutely not.'

'Not even if I promise to give you Nut Puffs?'

Ah, now that was a nasty one. A month ago, indeed a couple of weeks ago, she would have told him to stuff it, but now . . . she could do with that business, it would put her back on top for all to see. She needed a bit of, what did the French call it? *Signes extérieures de la richesse*.

She pulled herself together and did her best to look severe and composed. It was a stance that her features lent themselves to particularly well. Then he did for her completely.

'Shame about poor old Garramond, isn't it?'

'What? What's happened to him?'

Garramond was one of the main foundations of her power-base. She could sense the current tugging at her now, her arms starting to flail.

'He had a stroke this afternoon. Someone sent him one of those pop-up joke cards. Went badly wrong. Shock, I suppose. Just that little bit of extra strain. Taken to hospital, won't be back for months. If ever. Didn't like to tell you earlier. Thought it might spoil your evening.'

She wished people weren't so keen on not spoiling her evenings. She sat down. He poured her a drink.

'Now,' he said, 'gently squeezed or round and round?'

She started laughing. Could the cardiac have been caused by one of Howard's new designs? There was a certain irony in the idea. He had told her he'd sold a few prototypes to some local gift shop.

Bruce was a good if slightly shaming lover, although she knew the magazines said a sense of shame was the legacy of male-dominated sex. Whatever it was, it seemed to add a certain piquancy to the activity.

When he left, she poured herself another drink and wrote a letter to James saying she didn't want to see him any more.

They had always agreed, when and if they broke up, that they would never do it in writing.

17

Waking up on Saturday again at home, late and alone in the spare room, she experienced a particularly bad attack of weekend dread.

Why did she feel this way? Was it just a reaction after the adrenalin of the week? Or was it simply lack of local kindred spirits? For a couple of minutes' snooze-time, she thought about Martha.

Indeed, home would have undoubtedly been more fun with Martha around, but she and Trevor had moved three years earlier to a wing of an ugly old red-brick mansion in a coming area somewhere to the south-west of town.

It was nearer to Trevor's new job, which was nice for Trevor, but it had evidently been something of a blow for Martha. The day before they moved she had become quite emotional.

Charlet was by this time back at work and a Brand Manager to be watched, so they had already lost some of the day-to-day habit of the friendship, which was why she had been surprised at Martha's tears. The revelation that Martha was soft under the larky exterior was somehow unwelcome.

'Don't worry,' Charlet had told her lightly, 'we'll still see each other. Not so much perhaps. But when we do, we'll *stay* longer.'

Martha had clutched at her, and sniffed in a way that suggested she was going to Alcatraz rather than Bollingdon Park Executive Fine Homes A Buntrock Development. However, when Charlet made the pilgrimage to the new place, she found Martha had quite recovered her old sparkiness.

'You wouldn't believe some of the neighbours we have,' she told Charlet. 'They make the Crowthers seem positively mammalian. There's a man across the way who's bandaged his gatepost so his wife won't drive into it.'

'You're not serious?'

'Come and see.'

It was true. The wooden upright outside one of the converted stable units was padded and taped as if it were about to play centre for the Yankees.

'You'd think she was a sort of automotive Mrs Rochester,' said Martha.

Charlet looked at her with some surprise. It was the first time that Martha had ever expressed an interest in the classics, even as passing a one as this. Her friend noticed her raised eyebrows.

'It's my Literature Course,' she explained. 'When we

moved, I decided I had to do something with my life. So I enrolled. By the time I'm thirty-five, I'll have a Degree. That's something, isn't it? I've always resented the fact that I didn't go to university. Trevor's against it, naturally.'

'Naturally,' echoed Charlet, detecting another unfamiliar note in her friend's voice.

Martha and Trevor had always seemed to rub along reasonably well. This was the first time she had sensed real friction.

'You're so lucky to have children,' said Martha. 'We tried but we couldn't. My fault I'm afraid.'

They both stared moodily out at the swaddled gate.

'The funny thing is,' Martha suddenly remarked, gesturing at the stable unit, 'she can't drive.'

Charlet had enjoyed her day – it was pleasant taking up the easy handle of the old relationship – but she remembered wondering as she pointed the car down the over-generous dual carriageway between the Crematorium and the High School, whether the friendship would survive the extra mileage. And indeed, while it seemed to jolly along for a month or two, it became evident that the visits were growing more and more sporadic, the old easy banter getting increasingly clotted.

Neither of them said anything to the other. There would have been no point in drawing a line underneath the thing. No doubt there would be the odd merry meeting yet to come.

Indeed, so there was. But over the next three years, the meetings hardly doubled that figure. It seemed to suit both of them. Martha had her Course and Charlet her Career.

Lying in the spare room now, the past began to irritate her like a badly hung picture which she couldn't reach back and twitch into straightness. She got up and dressed without any sense of promise.

Later, reading the papers and drinking her breakfast coffee, her waking reveries seemed almost prophetic, for one of those odd coincidences occurred which indicate some pattern in life that, infuriatingly, one is forbidden to see. Martha rang up out of the blue.

'I'm taking the exam in a fortnight,' she said. 'Could I cadge lunch today? I need a break, and I could go on afterwards to collect some duvet covers from this amazing woman.'

Charlet's first instinct was one of impatience. Why couldn't Martha stay in her Green Belt waiting for their next birthday get-together? And then she wondered whether she couldn't use a friend.

'How lovely. Of course you can,' she said.

The memories of the old easy banter momentarily cheered her as she put the telephone down, but Howard came in to remind her that she had agreed to take the children out to lunch. Some long-delayed cartridge paper had arrived unexpectedly, and he had to collect it from the Customs Office at the airport.

The prospect of a pleasant gossip over vino receded.

'Couldn't Pentelle do it?' she asked.

'Pentelle's mother is sick. I don't want to bother her. She takes so little time off. Don't you want to take the children out to lunch?' he went on with irritating consideration. 'I'm sure we could ask the . . .'

'No, no, no. I'll do it.'

'I vote we go to the Boule de Suif,' said her son judiciously. 'One reads that their crêpes de fruits de mer are absolutely A-One.'

'But I wanted to go to La Capannina. You said I could go to La Capannina,' exclaimed his sister.

She liked the Capannina because the waiters flirted with outrageous punchinello sexuality.

'You chose last time, remember?' said her brother. 'If you wanted to go to La Capannina you should have gone last time. But you didn't. You went to La Lubianka instead and it was absolutely despicable.'

They finally agreed on the Boule de Suif and, when Martha arrived, they all huddled into Charlet's car and headed for a shopping centre a couple of miles away where the restaurant occupied a house of unobtrusive ugliness.

Inside, it was decorated like a French police station with disciplinary brown and cream glazed bricks. A low light from the faded lace-curtained windows did nothing to foster a sense of intimacy, while a single bulb in a wizened little shade overhead bounced messages of luminosity from wall to wall but failed to follow them up with any real glow.

There might have been one or two other people eating in the restaurant, but one couldn't count on it.

Charlet knew they had come to the wrong place as soon as they walked in, but there seemed no point in complaining. The children looked well content, and trotted forward expectantly. She shrugged wryly at Martha as they were led to a cheerless little table by a pale, prematurely-desiccated young waiter, and abandoned for the regulation anxiety-interval.

How different, she thought, from the evening of cuisine nouvelle with Bruce.

She stole another quirkily sympathetic look at her friend, but Martha was helping the children decipher the menu, which was the last thing they wanted.

Martha seemed to have grown larger. Perhaps it was the kaftan-y dress she was wearing, but she appeared to be positively swelling, not just with more Martha but with information and meaning. She started talking to the children about conservation and the bird count she had been doing for the local naturalists' trust in her Green Belt.

Watching her son looking at her friend with hostile

88

condescension, she realized that Martha was laughing too much.

'And you,' she was saying to them now, 'what are you interested in?'

'Food,' they replied as one.

'And wine, of course,' said Paul.

'Do you know the origin of the word "mayonnaise"?' Martha asked, roguishly. 'Bet you don't. Bet you anything you like you don't.'

'I'd like a hundred million pounds,' said Paul promptly.

'I'd like a hundred million billion trillion pounds,' said Natasha.

'Hoo hoo hoo hooo hoo,' laughed Martha.

'You'd better look out,' said Charlet, bored and nervous.

'It's derived from the town of Mahon,' said her son.

'In the Napoleonic Wars. They ran out of butter so they invented this sauce,' her daughter continued.

'Mahonnaise. Anyone knows that,' the boy observed scornfully. 'And now you're bankrupt. How galling.'

'If they'd had you two around they wouldn't have needed to invent it,' said Martha, shaking with mirth. 'You've got enough sauce of your own.'

The children spent ages choosing from the menu, caring nothing for the waiter's curling lip.

'What's the difference between a terrine de légumes and a timbale jardinière?' the boy asked him.

'"Oh timbaloo, how happy we are!"' carolled Martha.

'Why do you keep laughing?' the little girl asked her.

'This is quite a serious restaurant, actually,' said Paul

'The French are serious about their food,' the little girl confided.

'Oh, I say, gosh, sorry,' giggled Martha.

'You should have the gigglot of lamb,' said Natasha, pointing at the gigot on the menu.

The waiter wiggled his hip.

Charlet suddenly felt desperate.

'I'll have the salade frisée and the poussin,' she announced, choosing something harmless.

'Why don't you choose for me?' said Martha brightly to the children. 'But nothing too lumpy or red meaty, mind.'

Natasha and Paul went into a huddle, and finally ordered pâté de grive for her, followed by saumon à l'oseille.

'Oh, goody,' said Martha. 'Grive's a little town in the Dordogne, you know. One of my favourite places.'

Paul selected sea-food crêpes and maigret de canard for himself, and Natasha plumped for escargots and noisettes d'agneau.

The wine Paul ordered was a St Veran which he said was every bit as good as a more obvious choice like an expensive Chablis, and which indeed it turned out to be, after he had gone through an eery little ritual of nosing and swilling.

There was a long pause while they sipped their wine and mineral waters. The restaurant seemed once more to have gone into abeyance. Even Martha's jocularity dried up while the children discussed the merits of the wine list.

Some bizarre semblance of life was restored when an old man whom they had finally observed through the grey light very slowly eating moules in a far corner, was put into his coat and carried out.

'Tell me about the Course,' said Charlet, hopelessly.

'First course or second course?' queried the children.

'Martha's Course. She's taking an exam soon.'

Martha started to talk about semiotics. She spoke rapidly as if someone had pressed a switch. Finally the food arrived. Martha switched back to conservation, and started doing bird imitations.

Charlet picked at her food dubiously. You never knew

with the French. Martha, however, tucked into her pâté with a will, congratulating the children on its smoothness, and smearing it thickly on to her bread.

Charlet asked for some Perrier and, as the waiter placed the bottle limply on the table, Martha restrained him with a kaftaned arm.

'Tell me, garçon,' she said, 'what exactly is this smooth pâté that I am so much enjoying? I have never tasted anything quite like it.'

'That is a local delicacy of Provence, madame.'

Martha paused in mid-mouthful. Something in the waiter's manner made Charlet's stomach lurch.

'Of Grive, yes,' said Martha. 'But I thought that was in the Dordogne.'

'Grive not Brive, madame. Grive is not a place. It is a bird.'

'A bird? What sort of bird?'

One could hear the fringes of panic beginning to appear round Martha's voice. Charlet looked sternly at the children.

'It is a how you say . . .'

The children started to whistle 'too-too-too-tweet-twit' like little Papagenos.

'It is a thrush, madame,' the waiter concluded.

'Did you say thrush?' asked Martha, paling.

'But certainly, madame,' said the waiter with satisfaction.

'I have been eating thrush? This is all . . . thrush?'

The thrush was an endangered species in Southern Europe.

She picked at her little pot, and turned out a little dark section of what looked like truffle in the middle of it.

Before the waiter could reply, Charlet heard her son cut in.

'Especially that. That's the best bit of all.'

'What . . . what bit's that?'

91

'That's the thrush's song-box, don't you know?'

Martha made a muffled choking noise.

The rest of the meal passed quietly, apart from the appreciative slurps of the children. In the old days, reflected Charlet, she and Martha would have laughed at the whole stupid occasion. Now it was, in some peculiar way, cumbersome; even shameful.

When it was over, they said goodbye to each other as though nothing had happened.

'I'll be a bit tied up for the rest of the month,' said Martha, pale but now composed.

Charlet wished her luck. She didn't think she'd be seeing her again.

'Must have lunch soon.'

'Must.'

'Give us a call.'

'Will do.'

'Byee.'

'Fancy her not knowing what grief was,' said her daughter, afterwards. 'You knew, didn't you, Mummager?'

Charlet nodded absently, caught between disloyalty and the necessity of keeping her end up.

18

Three weeks later, Bruce took her up to the factory at Skelmington, a small town some three hundred miles to the north, to see a 'pilot' run of Nut Puffs being produced.

'You realize,' he had warned her jokingly, 'if you're going to take this one on, you'll be responsible for failure as well as success. It's been my baby up till now.'

'It's not going to be a failure. It's the apotheosis of

Fastfoods, the ultimate bubble. After this, the deluge,' she laughed.

She drove to the small airport, parked her Porsche (it was her new perk as Senior Group Brand Manager, part of the deal when she took on Nut Puffs), and joined Bruce in the Courtesy Lounge.

A light early morning mist was still clinging to the periphery, as if reluctant to expose the limitless vistas of suburb and golf course. One or two trees stood embarrassedly around behind the airport control buildings doing their best to keep out of the way of Senior Management preoccupations.

It was one of Bruce's sardonic mornings. (He had told her earlier that if they had an affair he would maintain a strict impartiality of manner towards her during working hours; more for her sake than his, he assured her.)

'Move your ass. We're late,' he said.

Evidently he had not heard of the Aquarian tendency. However, because of his habit of grinning when he was being offensive, it was difficult to take offence.

They clambered into the executive six-seater, and took off. A sewage works presented itself to their view as they banked sharply, and then climbed through cloud. Bruce went to sleep as the pilot emerged to ask her if she'd like to handle his controls, ha ha.

She declined but he stayed beside her telling stories about the life of a tame company pilot.

The journey could have taken half an hour or a day, it seemed to her an entirely relative matter, she did not want to go where she was going, equally she would have been upset to have been left behind. It was the kind of joyless ride executives had been invented for.

The plane sank through the clouds again, and landed beside another golf course. The assistant manager of the factory greeted them aromatically. You could smell the Nut Puffs clinging to his person.

'How's it going, Freddie?' said Bruce.

'Not so bad, Bruce,' said Freddie.

Pretty women obviously embarrassed him. Charlet knew that sexual equality had not yet gone far in the provinces.

The journey to the factory seemed to take them round and round the outskirts of several small towns. It was not designed to lift the spirits. The factory itself was a number of red-brick buildings in a disused railway marshalling yard behind a canal. As soon as they got out of the car, the air was heavy with Nut Puff effluvium. And Nut Puff fragrance billowed about them as they entered a door marked Reception.

Freddie provided Charlet and Bruce with a white coat apiece and an absurd toy-soldier cocked white hat.

'Would you like coffee first?' Freddie asked Charlet.

'No,' said Bruce, giving that particular smile which showed he knew she would've liked one. 'Better get on.'

'I'm afraid it's rather noisy in there,' said Freddie.

It wasn't the first time Charlet had been to a factory, of course. But her previous products had not demanded quite such an intensity of bubble-blowing. When Freddie opened the door, it was like being caught in a creeping barrage. Boom boom boomph. Boom boom boom BOOMPH.

'THE NUTS,' shouted Freddie, 'ARE FIRST OF ALL STRIPPED AND WASHED IN THIS ROTATOR.'

He pointed at a pit full of the intensively reared hazels from which the raw material of the Puffs was sublimed. The nuts streamed down an automated line supervised by grim white-turbaned women who occasionally dipped their gloved hands into the stream and walloped them about as if they were children. The river of kernels thus coaxed, thinned out as it approached a high-rimmed narrow mouth down which the hybrid cobs sped saying goodbye forever to conventional nutdom.

The huge aluminium churn wobbled and hissed, emitting from certain valves little runnels of sludge which seeped over the floor, discolouring Charlet's Italian shoes.

'SORRY,' bellowed Freddie, 'I SHOULD'VE GIVEN YOU GALOSHES.'

'Don't worry,' said Bruce, grinning like a death's head.

'YES PLEASE,' shouted Charlet – the shoes were particularly good ones – but Freddie and Bruce were already walking on down the line.

'THIS IS THE PULVERIZER,' shrieked Freddie, 'WHERE THE NUTS ARE CRUSHED AND AT THE SAME TIME HAVE ALL THEIR EXCESS MOISTURE REMOVED.'

A massive steam roller affair, poised over the production line, gobbled up the strange little round albinos as they surged endlessly forward. More liquid matter was emitted towards the front of the machine, this time a greasy grey porridge which, drying instantly, formed a soft crust around one of her ankles.

She walked towards the other end of the machine where a fine white powder hung in the air like spume over Niagara. A great flat white tapeworm now wriggled down the line into which Freddie dipped a little shovel, crying out to her to try it.

It looked revolting and tasted of nothing at all.

'NEXT WE ADD THE VEGETABLE OILS AND ARTIFICIAL COLOURING, PRESERVATIVES AND FLAVOURING.'

She thought of something.

'WHY DO YOU NEED TO ADD ARTIFICIAL COLOUR AND FLAVOURING WHEN YOU'VE JUST TAKEN OUT THE NUTS' OWN NATURAL ONES?'

'SORRY?'

'DON'T WORRY.'

Bruce looked at her and rolled his eyes, as though that

were just the sort of question not to ask technicians, how could she be so stupid?

They were gazing at a great steel hopper into which various mini-hoppers disgorged their burdens from above. Men in white overalls on Meccano galleries kept plying these jorums with canisters of numbered liquids.

Boom boom boomph. They were nearing the source of the explosions. Charlet felt a headache beginning to take shape. The tapeworm had now turned golden-brown and looked faintly tacky.

'TASTE IT,' yelled Freddie proudly.

Charlet looked at Bruce despairingly, but received no support. She dipped in Freddie's shovel tentatively; but Freddie, mistaking her aversion for diffidence, gallantly seized it from her and scooped her up a magnum-sized wedge.

'IT'S GOOD,' hollered Freddie, coming and going through her headache and the general uproar like a badly tuned radio. 'WE'VE INCORPORATED THE latest fragrANCE and FLAVOUR techNOLOGY including the pheromones of boom boom COPULIN to turn on MORE THAN THE TASTEBUDS!'

Charlet had read, of course, in the trade papers about the new flavouring experiments with pheromones, the aromatics based on human 'trigger' smells, but had assumed this was merely blue-sky futuristic research, nothing to do with anything she'd actually find on her own production line.

Now, however, was not the time for elucidation.

She took the piece Freddie was waving at her, and had a cautious nibble. It tasted of savoury praline, which wasn't so bad, but the trouble was that the flavour stayed on and on in the mouth like a sort of winsome kipper.

Nausea, once more a willing auxiliary, sprang to second her headache.

Boom booom BOOOMPH. BOOM BOOOM BOOOOOOMPH.

She pulled herself together. This, after all, was her prize project.

'AND HERE,' Freddie ranted on, endlessly enthusiastic, 'HERE IS WHERE WE ADD THE SPECIAL BINDING FACTOR, BASICALLY AN AGAR-AGAR DERIVATIVE, THAT HOLDS THE MIXTURE UNDER PRESSURES OF BOOOM BOOOM BOOOMPH PSI.'

This was the last stage in the worm's journey before it hit the guns. A treacly effluvium covered the housing of the cluster of hopperettes. It smelt of rank fish. She tried to wipe away a stray lock of hair which had fallen from her Simple Simon hat, and instantly her hair seemed full of the stuff.

Suddenly, she knew she was going to be sick again. Bruce seemed to have disappeared, and Freddie had moved forward to enthuse over the portion controller and the hot air nozzles which both cooked and inflated the ghastly mixture.

Spotting a nearby hopper, conveniently shoulder height, she was tempted to thrust her face in it and deposit her breakfast inside, but just in time spotted a door marked STAFF which led to a tiny lavatory. She threw up neatly . . . it was obligatory in the circumstances – and sat recovering with her head in her hands. Odd sensations of school assailed her. What would happen if she refused to come out?

She rejoined Freddie (no one seemed to have missed her) and gazed attentively while he outlined the intricacies of the Bofors-like appliances which injected the lozenges with white-hot air and then blew them down their barrels at ever so many feet per second. The BOOM BOOM was the hot air press going to work, the BOOOMPH was the shower of Puffs emitting from the orifices, Freddie explained rapturously.

'INCREDIBLE,' she bawled at Freddie, watching as the hopper into which she had wanted to puke was tipped by two masked myrmidons into the hopperettes where the binding process was effected.

Oh well, she thought, it would have been thoroughly cooked.

She couldn't, in all decency, jib when Freddie handed her a handful of the crispy-crunchy result, all hot from the guns.

It had to be admitted that the Nut Puffs, cooked, tasted a great deal better than they had raw, and doubtlessly infinitely better than crispy-crunchy spew. They were also prodigiously large in size, like great Honesty pods, and somehow the method of their cooking made them pop in the mouth with an extra crispy 'thock' of nutty flavour which would no doubt be heaven-sent to the advertising team that was eventually unleashed upon them.

She mused on these matters numbly as Freddie concluded the tour by showing the finished Puffs scuttling along to a thing like a nodding donkey which delivered exactly the right weight ratio into each plain foil bag, vacuum-sealed it with a kiss, and sent it forth to the warehouse pending the various next stages of sample and research.

'Now,' said Freddie, showing her through a door into an area of merciful quiet. 'How'd you like to see some of our backroom boys?'

'I'd rather see the chef.'

She wanted to talk to him about his choice of recipe.

'Chef? I'm sorry, I don't understand.'

'Don't you have a chef who sort of supervises the kitchen?'

'Kitchen?'

'I fear Charlet has somewhat romantic notions about

98

food,' said Bruce, suddenly emerging from a side-door whither he too had disappeared but not, she thought, for a weak puke, not he. 'She doesn't realize that chefs are part of the Dark Ages in terms of fastfood production. A pinch of this and a pinch of that. Faugh! Food today is science, Charlet, not fol de rol. And now Freddie's going to show us his chamber of horrors.'

'I'll introduce you to the Senior Chemist,' Freddie assured her.

19

He led them through a door into a laboratory full of Gulliver-like professors who, if not engaged in trying to extract sunbeams from cucumbers, were devoting their expertly educated talents to no less loony ends.

'We do research here on quality control. There is an optimum size for a Nut Puff. Too small and its integument is too tough. Too big and it becomes brittle, losing its crispy crunchy snappy crackly mouth sensation attributes. Of course, even on the best regulated production lines, things can and do go wrong. Show her your display, Arthur.'

One of the men in white coats flicked a switch and a wall alcove was illuminated full of neatly labelled exhibits which, if Hieronymous Bosch had ever thought of keeping a confectionery and snack-line stall, would most certainly have been candidates for his counter display.

There were evil blackened things, like blasted souls. There were hideously twisted and mutilated Puffs looking more like something that had been removed after an extensive autopsy. There was a shockingly long one, bulbous and contused at one end like a satyr's penis.

There was an enormous football-sized one covered with cankerous stigmata.

Each shelf provided fresh occasion for wonder and repugnance. And at the end there was an exhibit that, had she had a less onerous morning, would have excited a greater degree of her attention. It was a little heap of dust in a transparent pouch bearing the label QUERY FATIGUE?

The word she reflected, summed up her feelings precisely. Now, surely, it is time for lunch? And yet, even as the thought crossed her mind, she was surprised and a little shocked at herself. A month ago, she'd have been in there asking bright questions and leaving no freak unturned.

She thought she noticed Bruce looking at her strangely, but simply put it down to today's particular vein of games-playing. Her head felt as tight as Exhibit 32 – a Nut Puff that had miraculously achieved a near ceramic finish – and boom booom boomphed in time to the distant cannonade.

Lunch was in the Works Canteen, non-alcoholic and watery-stodgy. The steak pie pastry tasted of Puffs. The apple crumble appeared to have been crumbled with some of the less disturbing rejects from the Puff line. The very water carried its little flotsam of Puff powder which stuck to the glass. Only the coffee was Puff-less, but then it was undrinkable anyway.

Afterwards there was a short meeting to discuss the finished packaging, with a lively altercation between the protagonists of foil as opposed to see-through pouches; and then they were in the car skirting the huddle of grim little towns, and out on to the airfield again.

She deliberately sat in the corner of the plane furthest from Bruce, but he was suddenly in a vein of exceptionally charming humour. It was as if he had deliberately chosen to upset her during the visit, but now it was over he would treat her with all the taste and graceful bonhomie which were her due.

For a while, it was true, she was cool to him. But, when the pilot once again handed over to his opposite number, and came down to chat to her again, Bruce good-naturedly put him in his place.

'Bugger off, Splodger,' he told him, 'and see if you can't get us a drink out of that cabinet of yours. I want to talk to this very lovely colleague of mine.'

'I'd rather speak to Splodger, actually,' she said coldly, 'though I daresay he has a rather more polite name.'

'Well, no, actually,' said the pilot, 'I've always been called Splodger. I rather think I was christened Splodger as a matter of absolutely gospel fact.'

He also, it seemed, had a facility for tact, since it was not part of his job to put the backs of senior executives up.

'Lemon with your vodka and tonic?' he asked her.

'Please.'

He handed her a glass. She sipped and felt the spirit start to relax her.

'I'm afraid I haven't got any nibbles,' said Splodger, 'but I could do you some Nut Puffs if you like.'

'For crying out loud . . .' started Charlet and Bruce in unison.

20

The letter came to the office in an official envelope.

She had used the office address – for some reason she didn't want Howard to know about her search for her father.

It read quite simply: 'We have noted your enquiry re

news of father but regret that the mission he was engaged upon must still be classified as SECRET. Although actual evidence of your father's death has never been established, we have every reason to believe that he is, in fact, deceased and no foreseeable benefit can be envisaged in your further research. His disappearance occurred some time ago, at great distance from this country, in circumstances of the utmost danger. We assure you that his distinguished service has not been forgotten. We are, etc.'

It was signed by a squiggle, and had an official code-mark indicating the department it came from.

So that was it. She had politely been given the brush-off.

There were, however, elements in the letter that seemed to her to indicate discrepancies, to offer cause for hope. For instance, why were they so sure he had died when he had been at such a distance from reliable witnesses?

Charlet went to the office library and started researching world affairs of twenty years ago, around the time she guessed her father to have vanished. She realized that she was developing something of an obsession with the quest, even leaving work undone that in her new position she ought to have given priority to; but it seemed to offer, in a curious manner, a way out of her present uncertainties.

She now had two men working under her, and her group was handling more business than any other in the company. She ran the Porsche. She was well paid. The company magazine referred to her as 'our Golden Girl'. There was rumour of an Associate Directorship even sooner than she had dared hope.

Her success was now echoed in a surprising way by Howard.

Whereas previously, for years, the household had been

able to run on terms of reasonable affluence due to her considerable salary at Fastfoods, suddenly Howard made his breakthrough.

He had, of course, sold designs here and there to quality card houses. He had achieved a small local success with his first pop-up monster. But suddenly he sold the whole series to a massive retailing enterprise which was going into novelty cards for the first time.

All at once 'Howard's Horrors', as they were called, were popping up everywhere. Essentially they were variants on the same slavering travesty that had sprung at her out of the oven, only in the finished state, of course, they leapt at you out of an envelope.

The original local variant had done for poor old Garramond (this was now definitely established). But instead of diminishing its popularity, this accident had merely served to propagate its legend and increase its sales.

Howard had even printed a health warning on the bottom: DO NOT GIVE TO PEOPLE OF A NERVOUS DISPOSITION.

And now, to join the original monster, there were other mutations with witty lines to boot.

There was, of course, the spidery ghoul bearing the inscription, 'I spied ya with another woman.'

There was the bulb-nosed cyclops. 'I nose you loves me.'

There was an appalling fish-dog, creature of nightmare, carrying a get-well message. 'Sea you bark in circulation soon.'

And so on. The jokes themselves weren't all that funny – in fact the whole point was that they shouldn't be – but the way Howard had worked out the monsters, in mere card, was little short of genius. The creatures really seemed alive as they bounded at you out of the envelope.

Curiously, although she knew she should be thankful, or even proud, Charlet found this late triumph of her

103

husband's adding to the sense of unease that had lately crept into her life.

And it wasn't just unease.

She'd been getting one or two things uncharacteristically muddled recently. Her secretary had left to become an Assistant Brand Manager – it was the policy of the Company to promote from within but why they should have to swipe her secretary just when she needed her most was a mystery. Not that she could stand in her way, but the succession of temps that had filled in had been of quite limitless idiocy.

Pentelle seemed to be in the house from morning till midnight, and every spare inch of space was now taken up with more and more nightmarish hilarities; skulls clacked, jaws nipped, webbed feet unfolded from harmless sachets, monsters of every description slithered and crept, in varying stages of completion, across every bed and sofa, and even on occasion the bath and, yes, the bidet where Charlet had found a disgusting lobster thing hunched under the taps which crawled towards you when you turned on the water.

And then, of course, there was Poppy.

Charlet had told Bruce about her, more out of duty than enthusiasm, not expecting that anything constructive would be done. But not at all. He had sent for Poppy next day – without telling Charlet – and now Poppy was installed in one of the groups he supervised, and was, according to both Poppy as well as other sources, well on the way to becoming another success story.

'Not like you,' said Poppy, 'never as good as you.'

She saw them once together, walking up a sidestreet before lunch, talking animatedly and walking very close to each other. Charlet doubted whether Bruce would actually go to the lengths of trying to seduce her, but she was aware that if he did, Poppy would certainly put advancement before nicety. And men seemed to get a peculiar pleasure, she knew, from screwing best friends.

'You know, love,' she said to Charlet when they were having a drink one evening after work, 'he's a remarkable chap that man of yours.'

'Yes?' said Charlet. 'I'm not sure that I like him though, really.'

'He knows you think that,' said Poppy, earnestly. 'It hurts him, you know. He's really sensitive underneath.'

There was something so irritating about the way she said it – as if Bruce of all people needed championing – that Charlet wanted to put a lobster up her frock.

21

After they'd returned from the visit to the Nut Puff factory, Bruce had another trip to make.

One of Fastfoods' overseas offices developed a critical path crisis. Bruce was on permanent stand-by as one of the senior management trouble-shooters, and critical paths were his speciality – particularly, it seemed, when the overseas office happened to be in an exotic location.

Before he left, he enjoined Charlet with great seriousness, in her office, with his tape-recorder recording to show just how serious it was, to clear her desk and really get behind the Nut Puff project. Not that she needed enjoining but he did it all the same.

Then to her relief, and surprise at her relief, he was gone.

To launch a major new brand for a large organization requires the meticulousness of a termite with the organizational capacities of a Cheops; the vision of an Isaiah with the patience of a Job. At least, so said the Company marketing manual in a rare patch of purple.

She had launched products before, of course; but never on such a scale; and never so fast.

Pack designs and copy had to be approved – the design outfit had already come up with twenty-eight different designs, out of which a short-list of three was made, and each of these had to be exhaustively researched.

The advertisement programme itself had to be discussed, presentations made, pilot commercials reviewed on animatic; and these too had to be tested and shown to small panels of housewives.

The product itself had to be monitored and tested for shelf-life, although this part of the programme had to be streamlined since, according to Bruce, there was so much pressure from the top for the launch to be brought forward.

There was promotional material to be organized. The sales side had to be consulted and made to feel they were in on the act and altogether suitably hyped-up; the production department had to be given forecasts; the warehouse people needed both short- and long-term briefing; the 'below the line' team required notice of how much money was going to be available for competitions, on-pack promotions, coupon redemption exercises, and shelf-wobblers.

There simply wasn't enough time in the day. Because she was so often working late, she found she was having to spend more time in the Waiting Room, even though instinct and Larry's Law said it'd be a good thing to put in a little more time at home right now, monsters or no monsters.

Her fatigue helped her in her resolution to see no more of James, though he still kept cropping up on her doorstep. On these occasions, she would politely but firmly push him out into the night.

Sometimes he would cry. She found this awkward, though it didn't dent her determination.

'You hard-hearted bitch,' he sniffed. 'I've practically told Susie I'm leaving her.'

'Practically,' she said, 'but as usual not quite. The trouble with you, James, is not so much that you're weak, but that you think everyone else in the world is equally feeble. Go and find someone as morally sloppy as you are. The fact is, even if you did leave her, I wouldn't have you back.'

It was hard on him, but she felt the situation called for it. Enough was enough.

'You'll rue the day,' he said, 'one day you'll come crawling, and you know what I'll do?'

'Spurn me with your shoe?'

'I wouldn't stoop.'

'Spurning with the shoe does not involve crouching.'

'How can you be so cruel?'

'Look James, I'm sorry but I've got work to do. Bugger off, would you?'

It was on one of these occasions that Bruce suddenly appeared, clutching a bottle of champagne.

'Oh Charlet, I just got back and wondered if . . .'

He took in the scene, the door still open, Charlet red-faced, the man tearful.

'Is this man disturbing you?'

'No, no. It's all right. He's a friend, I suppose.'

'I'm glad about that. Otherwise I might have had to wrap his neck around the lamp standard.'

'You what?' said James truculently – he was a little drunk as usual. 'You and who?'

'Look, sonny, I'd just disappear if I were you.'

Charlet started to bob between them like a boxing referee. Bruce turned to her suddenly.

'Did I ever tell you about my spell in the Marines?'

He made one or two chopping movements with his

hands. James blinked. He was not really a fighter, at least not with other men.

'I've a good mind to . . .' he blustered, but stopped when Bruce took a step towards him.

'Very well,' he went on. 'I see. The air seems to have thickened. The situation seems to have become obtuse. I don't know who this person is but he seems to me to bear all the hallmarks of a maths master!'

Charlet knew that James hated maths masters and regarded them as the worst species of sadistic bully, having been troubled by them in his youth. Bruce was clearly puzzled by the expression, but caught the general drift.

'Are you calling me a maths master?' he asked unnecessarily. 'Call me a maths master again, and you'll find yourself up shit creek. Turn out your pockets.'

'What?'

'I said, turn out your pockets. I want to see the filthy state of your pockets.'

He strode over to James and with a single gesture shook the contents of his jacket on the floor as if he were undressing him.

'What did you do that for?' asked James, more shocked than angry.

'You called me a maths master. I acted like a maths master. You are clearly terrified of maths masters. Now you are terrified of me.'

There was no arguing with Bruce when he was in this mood. Indeed, as she looked at him, she thought there was indeed something of the maths master about the man, an air of having effortlessly learnt some hidden trick or secret that made the knotty calculations of life easy, but that somehow didn't make him happy, just more impatient of others.

She felt that funny tremor of apprehension again.

It was suddenly like being caught out late in a forest,

familiar hunting by day, but now full of little rustlings and trepidations she'd never noticed before.

James cast a despairing look at her, collected up his scattered pens and address-book (she almost expected to see crumbs and a white mouse), and stumbled numbly down the stairs.

The whole incident was ludicrous, and yet you could never be quite sure whether Bruce was acting out of a sardonic impulse or was quite simply sadistic, liking to inflict humiliation by creating absurdity.

The laughter that welled up in her was partly an expression of apprehension unrelieved by James's departure.

'I don't think he'll come snivelling around here again,' said Bruce, opening the champagne, 'anyway, he's not your type. Only mix with the best. That way some of it rubs off.'

'You have a high opinion of yourself,' she said.

'If I don't, how can I expect anyone else to have? At least fifty per cent of Fortune is self-generated.'

'And the other fifty?'

'That is Fortune's wheel. But on the whole she's a bully. She goes for the weak.'

'It takes one to know one.'

'Drink your champagne and stop bitching.'

The champagne was very cold.

'Pins and needles on ice,' she said.

Later he poured a little river of it down her pubic hair so it trickled inside her, fizzing impishly, and he drank it greedily like a dog.

Later, when he had gone, she dreamt that she was lying on the bed, touching herself in front of him, while he took pictures of her with a small pop-up flash camera which turned into one of Howard's monsters, obscenely alive.

She came with a great surge of guilty delight, and woke up.

She had the sudden terrifying feeling that there was somebody in the flat. It was pitch-dark. In the distance, a car licked wet tarmac. Something on the river hooted mournfully. In a panic, she lunged over and upset the bedside light. Finally she managed to switch it on. The familiar dimensions of the room revealed themselves. The door was on the latch. The half-drawn curtains billowed in the draught from the opened window. Down in the street something knocked over a dustbin lid.

A terrific sense of loss swept over her.

The first grey light of morning pressed against the window, wan yet persistent, like unwanted memory.

22

The two Brand Managers working in her Group were in one way similar – neither was what she would have chosen in ordinary circumstances.

The manner of their appointment to her team still rankled, since it was generally recognized that Senior Group Brand Managers had the choice of their own appointees. But, because of the urgency of the Nut Puffs project, there had not been time to assemble the team in the customary manner. Even if there had been, she was by no means sure that Bruce would have let her. Indeed, she had taxed him with it one evening.

He had jokingly pretended that he was jealous, that he didn't want her to have a stud of young rams on her team, that he was just trying to get her Group organized and operative with a minimum of fuss for her, that he wished her to have tried and tested people aboard who'd give her experienced support. However, she knew that, with Bruce, things were never that simple.

Perhaps he really was jealous, but didn't want her to know it, simply pretending to be devious. Perhaps he wished to seem jealous. Perhaps there was an altogether different reason which she couldn't even guess at.

'They may be experienced,' she complained, 'but that doesn't actually mean they're any good.'

'You'll lick them into shape, Charlet,' he said, 'it's all a matter of leadership.'

It was hard to counter a challenge like that. Fastfoods were very hot on Leadership. It was the Managing Director's favourite theme after Decision.

Meanwhile, she had Bryan Hinkley and David Kesler on her hands.

Apart from the similarity of their appointment, they could hardly have been more disparate.

Bryan was long and cadaverous with frizzy brown hair and teeth that didn't quite seem to fit the shape of his lips, always closing with a click before his mouth did, especially when he had finished smiling. He smiled a great deal without any causative element of humour. It was a sort of reflex expression derived from his sense of the wonderfulness of being Bryan.

He was almost unbelievably lacking in any power of intuitive appraisal.

He would talk round a problem endlessly, and give you all manner of bouncily logical reasons why such a thing should be, and if you were tired you could almost be persuaded by his rubberiness of reasoning that he was right. And then he'd say something so totally stupid that you were saved at the last moment from agreeing with him.

The only thing was, just occasionally he had a good idea but you tended to discard it along with everything else he said.

When Bryan had first arrived at Fastfoods from Sunbeaker, it had been generally reckoned that his stay with the company would be transitory, but somehow he had remarkable powers of survival.

'Bryan's so absurd no one feels threatened by him,' she had told Penny when she was giving her a rundown on some of the people in the organization, though she now began to feel, at least on her own behalf, that she might want to qualify the opinion.

At all events, the man had an astonishing ability to spring back after what many people would have considered humiliating reverses. He reminded Charlet of a toy she'd had as a child: the Wobbly Codger. It had a fatuous grin and a lead-weighted base, and always reverted to the perpendicular no matter how hard the knockdown.

The other man in her Group, David Kesler, was as small and compact as Bryan was long and elasticated.

He was probably Jewish. His age was unguessable.

He could look thirty. At other times, his hooded expression seemed to convey the accumulated wisdom of many decades. He had little black glittery eyes, dark hair, a white face. He always wore a black suit with a white shirt. The general effect was that of an elderly civil servant with a penchant for playing Lord Fauntleroy.

David did not make mistakes, but he sometimes encouraged others to do so – at least that was his reputation. He might 'forget' to tell you something that would have made all the difference to your presentation. He might see that you mysteriously did not receive an important memo until it was too late to act upon it.

In fact, thought Charlet when she heard the news that she was to get him, he was a dangerous little snake, and only the 'leadership' challenge prevented her slinging him back to Special Projects, where he had been one of Bruce's protégés.

He was said to live with an aged mother, and never went out with girls; at least that was the word from the Programmers, and they usually knew.

When she had repeated all this to Bruce, he had been quite exercised on the subject.

'The fact is, he's brilliant, Charlet. People are frightened of him because he has a first-class mind. Look at the work he did on Savoury Fidgits. Just a bit awkward with women, that's all. Being in your Group may actually help him there. You can't expect everything on a plate, you know, Charlet. The higher you go, the harder it gets.'

'I don't expect everything on a plate. It'd just be nice not to have everything with sand and dogshit all over it.'

Charlet had never appealed to his decencies as a lover during their working day, it was part of the unspoken agreement, but she was beginning to suspect that the reverse applied. It was because she was his lover that he was behaving in this crabby way. She wasn't even going to ask him why. She knew what he would say.

'I don't want people to think that I'm favouring you, Charlet.' That would be his line.

And she knew, however much she might like to believe it, that it would not be true.

Bruce's face now took on a more severe and authoritative demeanour.

'Kesler is very far from being dogshit, Charlet. And I wouldn't say things like that to his face. I am told he can be sensitive. You must try to seem a little less paranoid about everything. If you feel the responsibility's too much for you, you only have to say so. I am told they are looking for senior people in D & L.'

Diabetic and Laxative lines occupied the same kind of status in Fastfoods that Asia Minor enjoyed under Tiberius.

She didn't mention dog business to Kesler in any shape

113

or form, but she got the feeling that somehow he'd heard about it already. She could sense his glittery little eyes on her sometimes as she bent to check a report or stood against a window in a silk blouse, a gaze not sexual but a spy's, measuring her up and putting her down on microfilm to be analysed later.

Of the two, Charlet felt she'd rather be betrayed than made to look an idiot, though the two might well come to the same thing, so she gave most of the work on the Nut Puff project to Kesler.

Their first job was to put together a detailed plan of campaign for the launch, having gathered every possible scrap of information that could be indicative.

A research executive, weary with omniscience – he'd seen them come, he'd seen them go – went through the latest sampling findings with them. Even he was forced to admit that there seemed a wide level of acceptance both on a socio-economic and on an age and sex paradigm.

He showered them with charts that indicated the savoury craze, the Swing from the Sweet, as he put it, which had gripped the nation for a decade, that there was now evidence of a swing towards a more 'natural' sweet-alternative savoury product.

Hazelnut was seen by people as a reminder of their youth, of country values, of expensive praline chocolates (the three were not by any means incompatible); while the bubble image, as they already knew, was accepted by weight watchers, young adults, children and for some reason pregnant mothers, and Fastfoods had already spent many millions of pounds on making it so.

Normally there would have been a test-market in a selected town, but Charlet felt that more was expected of her than the usual red tape, and indeed Bruce had more or less implied that the Company rather anticipated a more ambitious approach from her.

114

So, at the first meeting of the new Group's Plans Board, she decided to make her pitch straight away.

'I'd like to go national with this one,' she said assertively.

Bryan opened his mouth, and closed it again with a click. David merely turned and gazed at her with his little black pruney eyes.

There was a pause. Then Bruce, with a show of diffidence that was entirely arrogant, stuck his oar in.

'The Marketing Director had asked me merely to keep a watching brief on this one, Charlet. The decision must be yours, of course. But I can't help feeling it might be prudent to exercise our usual disciplines.'

He might want to allay any suspicion that he was favouring her, but he didn't have to pull the whole rug out. She countered strongly.

'I hear what you say, Bruce, of course, but isn't there another dimension to this? If we delay, we could lose business worth, what? a couple of million. And be pipped by Inter-Baker, who I hear are developing a crackle which is basically a Nut Puff me-too, apart, of course, from being flat. A sort of Mercator's projection of a Puff, you might say.'

No one laughed. Charlet ploughed on.

'If we brief the ad agency now, we could have a TV commercial by next month . . . we could hold a Special Sales Conference a week later . . . well, in say another three weeks . . . we could have it on the market by . . .'

'I don't like launches post-holidays,' said Kesler.

'For Chrissake, David, let's try and stretch the rules a bit, shall we? If we wait, we're going to have to share the limelight with the other guys. Post-holidays, people want a bit of a treat. All that feasting and rich food . . . what could be more appropriate than a savoury bubble?'

'What d'you say, Bryan?' asked Bruce.

'I'm rather reminded of a sausagette product we

115

launched at Quick-Fare,' clicked Bryan, and launched into one of those long irrelevant excursions round his past, concluding: 'After two weeks in the outlets it started to twist into the most extraordinary shapes, quite suggestive some of them. People, especially females, got shy of asking for them, not that it affected the flavour but we had to take the whole lot back.'

He grinned like a letterbox and clicked shut.

'I think Bryan's point is shelf-life, Charlet. Any problems there? Do we know the product well enough for a national launch?'

'I . . .'

She remembered the factory and its chamber of horrors. But they were all freaks of the development stage, weren't they? Nothing had been said about contortion proneness. Besides she couldn't very well back down now.

'I'm confident of our team up there, uh Bruce. That's one hell of a good product we're talking about.'

Bruce smiled like a leopard.

'I'm glad you're so confident, Charlet. But I think I'm going to have to override you on this one. We'll take a test town. Gomborough, I think.'

Charlet could hardly believe her ears. Bruce had been the one who'd been urging her to go for the big time, and now here he was publicly eroding her authority.

Kesler stole a glance of malicious amusement at her, and Bryan's teeth performed a veritable tap-dance before they finally slammed shut.

Charlet could feel the blush spreading across her face like a jellyfish sting.

'But, I . . .'

'Oh come on, Charlet. We all have to learn how to lose gracefully.'

'I don't mind losing,' she wanted to say, 'it's being knifed in the back that's so hard to get used to,' but instead she mustered a smile and said wrily: 'I suppose the safe option always has its attractions.'

It was Bruce's turn to colour. He prided himself on his forthright and positive stance, and disliked being shown up in front of juniors.

'Good,' he said, 'well, that's settled. We can start the test in three weeks' time. Now I don't think we need detain David and Bryan any longer. They have plenty to do. We don't want any booboos on this one. It's make or break time for all of us.'

It was the first time that Bruce had given any intimation that his head too was on the block. Did he mean it, or was he just including himself in their boat as a mark of good leadership?

Not for the first time, she kicked herself for allowing him to make love to her when every instinct had told her it would be a mistake. The trouble was, his particular style of lovemaking, lewd though it was, had become strangely necessary to her.

She stood there looking at him after the others had left, not knowing whether she was elated or miserable, anxious or interested.

It was as if she were on a Big Dipper with that half-ghastly sensation in the stomach that made you want to keep riding. She opened her mouth to protest at his cavalier behaviour, but he stopped her with one of his irritating non-smiles. She decided to regain the initiative.

'You bastard,' she said. And then: 'I bet you don't have the guts for a screw.'

'What? Here?'

'Right here.'

He locked the door, took the phone off the hook, and they made love on the office floor to the moody castanetting of the typewriters outside, with the shapes of the executives in the next office looming and dissolving in the frosted glass partition like cows in a fog.

A little stain on the regulation beige tufted-pile carpet remained as a savoury testimony to the encounter.

It was the only tangible result of her initiative.

23

Paradoxically, although Poppy was now working in the same building, Charlet saw less of her.

Once or twice she suggested a drink or evening out as in the old days but Poppy excused herself, saying she was working late, she had so much to catch up on, Charlet was way ahead of her, she could do things without thinking that she, Poppy, would have to spend hours working out.

However, Charlet finally managed to pin her down, and they went to a cocktail place, the Koolibar, run by a couple of expatriate Australian gays, that had recently become fashionable with the advertising agencies.

She wanted to tell her about a second letter she had received from the Ministry.

'They're so cagey,' she said to Poppy after they'd found a spare booth, and ordered their regulation delicacies. 'All I wanted to find out was his last known address. They've finally come up with one after sitting on their fannies for three weeks. Of course, it's twenty years since he was there, but I've looked it up in the street guide. It's down by the river in the Old Town. I want you to come with me and have a look.'

Poppy would normally have jumped at the notion, but now she put on her preoccupied executive expression.

'Oh, love, you know I'd adore to but,' she said, sucking at her Wallbanger as though it might be snatched away before she'd finished – a contingency which in view of the careless self-attention of the bobble-hatted waiters was in fact a prevalent one at the Koolibar.

A good-looking young executive Charlet recognized from the advertising agency came over, and she was preparing to freeze him off when he surprised, indeed shocked her by addressing Poppy first.

'Hullo, Pops,' he said.

Poppy gave a little wriggle as though her knickers had suddenly acquired a lover's knot.

It was almost the first time in Charlet's experience that a personable male had ignored her in favour of her friend. She took another look at Poppy.

The former scrawiness had filled out, and the neat business suit, cunningly altered, allowed a generous glimpse of executive thigh – Poppy had always had good legs, it was her best point. Assiduous waxing had disguised a tendency to bristle, and now they twinkled merrily at the adman as she invited him to join them, parting slightly in anticipation of his client-service attentions.

Charlet suddenly noticed just a scintilla of a smell of fish, that tenacious and erotic-disgusting aroma that matures after lovemaking. She looked around to make sure that kedgeree or Arbroath smokies weren't being served at the next table, but nothing remotely marine disturbed the arrangements of glasses and silver ashtrays where two young girl copywriters were discussing their latest salary increase; only a couple of saucers of what looked like Fastfoods' new Cocktail Baubles.

Fastidious to a fault, she could hardly believe that she herself was the source of such a thing; but Bruce had paid another visit to her office that afternoon, and she simply had to go down to the powder room to check.

No, there was nothing. She knew she had washed well in the executive bathroom. She smelt of vetiver soap and Italian perfume. Perhaps it had been, after all, a passing cobber with a dish of monkfish canapés. Or could it perhaps have been Poppy?

There had been something ticklishly guilty about her friend's demeanour that, the more she thought about it, convinced her that she indeed was the origin. What was going on in Fastfoods? In spite of her own behaviour in the office, she suddenly felt a surge of indignation. It was a surprise they got anything on the market at all. The place was like Gomorrah on a particularly busy night.

She looked at herself in the glass, feeling that the pressure that was beginning to build up around her temples must be echoed by some appearance of strain in her face, but she looked almost irritatingly the same. Her mouth, which had been mumbled heavily by Bruce, looked perhaps a little more bruised than usual, but it lent perhaps an extra touch of delinquence to the so-ordered features.

So what was wrong with her? Did she smell not of fish but, worse, of failure, like those ageing middle-management men she'd written off as lovers at all those sales conferences?

The fear that had been haunting the hinterland of her subconscious suddenly sidled out into the open. She decided that she must seduce the young executive upstairs. She didn't particularly want him, she knew it would offend Poppy, but she needed to prove that she was the desirable one she'd always been.

She sprayed on some more Missoni, patted her hair and went upstairs again.

The pair had gone, haddock-scent and all. Charlet could hardly believe that her friend – whom she had been perfectly willing to upstage – could have let her down so badly.

Out of the corner of her eye, she saw a small man with hair brushed sideways across his bald patch edging towards her.

24

Poppy was briefly apologetic next day when she bumped into her nibbling something in the whimpering lift under the pale gaze of Luddington, who was going through a silent mode.

'Sorry about that,' Poppy said, 'but it was a case of lust at first sight.'

She spoke as though lust were an excuse for every other offence, like drunkenness in the Army.

Luddington closed his eyes as if in prayer.

What if there really were something fishy in the Puff formulation? thought Charlet. The implications were truly cosmic. And yet, what could she possibly do about it if there were? The last thing she wanted to do was call her own pet project into question. She decided to say nothing to her friend.

'Bye, love, must fly, got to interview a man,' said Poppy. 'Must have lunch soon. 'Byeee.'

She scuttled off down the corridor with a busy twirl of pleats. Charlet suddenly had the feeling that Poppy knew more than she let on.

'The higher they rise,' said Luddington, suddenly communicative, 'the harder they fall. How d'you make a thin man fat?'

'I don't know, Luddy. How?'

'Throw him over a lift shaft and he comes down plump.'

25

She had maddeningly stalled the Porsche on one of those down-town junctions near the Waiting Room – she hadn't quite got used to the clutch, and anyway she was wearing the wrong sort of heels – and then it had refused to start again.

It was raining and she had had a bad day. There had been a sort of tremor of malice in the office that reminded her of school. It was as if everybody knew something that she didn't.

It was ridiculous, of course, because she had nothing to fear. She was far better at her job than most of the cringing backbiters that drank in Buddies Wine Bar after work; but it was still unsettling. And it was doubly unsettling to sit there conspicuously stalled in the dribble of the late rush-hour traffic where any of the gloating coterie might drive by.

She tried the starter again. The engine turned. The exhaust hubble-bubbled. But nothing else happened. She pumped the accelerator impatiently, little quirks of anger and misgiving beginning to register. She wanted a bath. She was meant to be meeting Bruce at a party.

'FAAA . . .'

He was pressing his lips to the glass in hideous close-up, and scrabbling at the door handle.

For a long moment, she was too shocked to do anything. He began to push at the panel of the door, and she could feel the car rocking as he put his weight to it.

The movement broke her paralysis. She couldn't remember whether the door was locked, and flung herself across the seat, hurting her breast on the handbrake.

In response to her lunge, she saw the Ancient Mariner figure start stumbling round to her side of the car. She noticed he had something wrapped in a newspaper in his hand. A bottle? Would he try to smash it against a window? Would it break?

She desperately struggled back again to the driver's seat. The creature was right beside her now, baleful and menacing, the white hair of his stubble giving his bloated features a strange demonic, electric quality.

'FAAA . . . FAAAA . . .'

He was grabbing at the door handle with one hand, and threateningly waving his parcel in the other. She was sobbing with fear now. How did the driver's door lock? She knew it – of course she knew it – but the surge of adrenalin had suppressed all reason.

The claw-like hand pulled at the handle, and the door started to open.

Sprawling inelegantly, gasping with fear, hands out-stretched to push him away, she retreated across the gear lever and brake again to the passenger side.

The figure loomed in, reeking of cheap spirit and unwashedness; arms plucking, mouth mumbling. She couldn't even remember how to open the door now. She was trapped. It had to be a knife, not a bottle, in that bundle. She realized she was going to be killed.

Just at that moment, she heard a familiar voice beside her.

'Having a little trouble with the new jalopy, Charlet?'

It was Bamstead, one of the Brand Managers who drank in Buddies Bar, passed over for promotion in favour of herself.

The tramp straightened up at his approach, and now backed off muttering and gesturing.

Bamstead looked in at her, smiling coolly as she tried to smooth her dress and look as though she had been reaching for the bonnet catch or the instructions manual

123

or a particularly modish cassette or anything really rather than this posture of indignity and distress.

'The . . . bloody thing's . . . stalled on me,' she told him, climbing out and looking at her pride and joy with disgust.

Bamstead climbed in with practised arrogance.

'Hairy motors, these,' he said, and switched on the ignition.

The engine started immediately.

'Not exactly a woman's car, I'd have thought,' he continued. 'Wouldn't you be better off with something smaller? That old fungus-face could've made off with all those Confidential files I see you've got stashed in there. Bruce would smack botties for that, and I wouldn't let it get as far as Affleck. There's a big thing about security at the moment what with all these new products coming along.'

He would make sure that everyone knew about it tomorrow.

'D'you want me to drive you home?' he went on, still sitting in the car.

She was feeling cold as well as mortified.

'No. No, thank you. It's fine now. Thank you for helping out.'

Get out of my car, you unctuous little prick, and let me get on my way.

'Think nothing of it. Damsel in distress and all that. Just so long as you're all right?'

'I'm fine, thank you.'

Was she going to have to haul him out?

'Wouldn't want our Golden Girl to get egg on her face.'

He smirked up at her, both lascivious and condescending.

'I really must be getting on, now.'

There was no point in being angry with him. It would

124

merely add relish to his feast. Baulked of the satisfaction, he swung himself out of the Porsche, and tried a last bout of solicitude.

'There's nothing that excites weirdoes more than pretty girls in smart cars,' he said. 'Sure you don't want me to drive home after you?'

Perhaps he imagined she would offer him a drink when they got there. Even if the idea had remotely appealed to her, which it didn't, she could just hear him boasting in Buddies to all his cronies about the way she had entertained him.

She seated herself resolutely in the car, and started the engine, revving it impatiently to indicate that the interview was about to be closed.

'Don't bother,' she said. 'I'm fine, really.'

But still he lingered.

'Sure?'

She nodded vigorously, and he finally let go of the Porsche's roof and started wandering off to his regulation executive saloon, turning to blow an impertinently ironic kiss as she drove off.

'I'm fine,' she repeated to herself.

But was she? Who was that tramp? What did he want with her?

Why had the stepping stones over which she had formerly tripped with such dexterity and lightness, suddenly started to squirm and tilt?

26

Though shaken by the episode, she decided on reflection next day that it at least had the merit of being a matter of fact.

Those other experiences she'd had (there had been one or two more since the incident of the oi-oi accident-resistant window-cleaners) were unsettling since they had gone on entirely in her head.

There had been the mother with the small boy in a push-chair, and the bus that had passed dangerously close but not quite struck them. It certainly hadn't burst a tyre as she had anticipated. And then there had been the young couple on that windy day as they passed under an old tree. No branch had fallen. And the aeroplane as it came in losing height over the city in the rain . . .

She had happened to mention it to the local curate who was also Fastfoods' Visitor. His only function was really to mastermind the annual carol concert round the Christmas tree in the vestibule, but he made a token appearance every Friday when he would hang around one of the ante-rooms, voraciously helping himself from the trays of courtesy snackadoodles.

He was taken aback to be consulted on such a shadowy matter, and rather gave her the impression that he thought pretty women with successful jobs had no right to have problems of any kind. His main concern was the uncaring nature of Society, and he put it to her that this might well be hers too. She was, he suggested, a very caring person with no real outlet. He urged her to join his Action Group.

Her doctor prescribed a mild tranquillizer that made

her feel woolly after lunch. If that didn't help, he told her, he could recommend a good psychiatrist but that would mean a six-month course of two sessions a week, which would involve really a very great deal of money.

He indicated, without saying it, that he thought there was absolutely nothing wrong with her.

Since money was more important than anything – the reason why she worked, the passport to something never fully defined but infinitely promising – she felt she could probably manage, after all, to cope with the experiences which were, in their rather disagreeable way, interesting – and free. As for the old tramp, perhaps she had been a little hysterical. He'd only wanted money to buy himself another drink.

Meanwhile she had work to do. The Nut Puff project was accelerating. There were pack proofs to be checked, more research to be evaluated, critical paths to be pursued.

Her affair with Bruce was now reduced to little more than sex. A Puff-like activity, appetite without satisfaction. She was torn by shame and desire, the one making the other more piquant, and she couldn't give it up.

Indeed, even if she had wanted to do so, it would have been impolitic to give Bruce the push until the launch had been successfully concluded.

Aware that her own libido seemed to have taken a lurch in a more than usually active direction, and with Freddie's muffled comments at the factory in mind, she asked Bruce one day if the experiments with trigger tastes and smells had ever been tried on company personnel.

Bruce immediately became pompous.

'It was wrong of Freddie even to mention it,' he said with official gravity. 'The whole thing's very much in the air.'

'In the air inside the bubble?' she enquired.

She found her very humour these days becoming brittle;

taut and Puff-like. Bruce didn't find her humour humorous at all.

'I must ask you not to mention it again – not to me and certainly not to anyone else. You know how these things get out. We don't want UniSnack getting wind of it.'

'But is it true?' she persisted.

Bruce became impatient.

'Oh for God's sake, Charlet. You know what the professors get up to. Dismiss it from your mind.'

But she found that she could not. The notion of copulin, distributed like fluoride, accumulating in the body corporate, began to obsess her.

The whole office, now that she thought about it, was fizzing with lust. Could it be that they were being monitored, part of some monstrous research programme, today Fastfoods, tomorrow the water supply? Those men who had come to measure her office for a new carpet – were they in fact wiring for sound, checking for stains? Was Bruce, privy to the secret, simply using her body for Company as well as for personal reasons?

The notion was, of course, too ridiculous; but she was positive she'd heard Freddie say those things at the factory, and Bruce seemed so unreasonably touchy about it. In a nightmarish way, the whole thing seemed to add up.

And yet, for some reason, perhaps like that of a drinker who is only too aware of his illness but wants a drink all the more, her inside knowledge merely served to inflame her for the evenings with Bruce.

The other consideration that haunted her, deflecting her attention from the pressing matter of the launch, and encouraging her to hand over more and more of its day-to-day administration to David Kesler, was the mystery of her father.

As each day passed, and the pressures surrounding her continued to accumulate, she found herself positioning him as if he were a product: a brave and gentle three-dimensional parent, tweedy and perhaps even pipe-tobacco-y, targeting at female executives needing a bastion in the shifting world of bubbles, monsters, shadows, stains, aromatics.

At the same time, she began to nurture the feeling that, because of her long neglect – the absence from her thoughts, the almost wilful negation of his memory – she was in some way responsible for his disappearance.

It was silly, she knew, she couldn't really be held to blame, but the longer she dwelt on it, the more the notion grew – he might still be alive, friendless, ill, destitute.

If only she had the time, she'd go down to that old address of his and see if anyone remembered him. The best she could do at the moment was to ask Information and Records about the area.

After a pause, during which her enquiry was processed, she was told that the district had first grown impoverished, then notoriously rough, and at last more or less run down in preparation for the demolition that was to resurrect the entire quarter as the new River City South East.

The more she heard, the more the journey seemed unlikely to be fruitful. But she felt she had to get round to trying. She owed at least that to him. The trouble was, the days at the moment simply weren't long enough, even though she had delegated to Kesler, who now reported to her on shelf-life, production dates, warehousing, distribution. For all his faults of personality, he was at least intelligent, thorough and organized. It certainly took some of the pressure off her, but it still meant she was putting in a ten- or eleven-hour day.

As for Bryan, who was a kind of machine for creating extra work and should have been employed by the government, she could keep an eye on him on the packaging and promotional fronts where much of the actual output was anyway done by others – advertising men, public relations people, packaging department, print buyers.

A pack design had by now been agreed and printed, since the critical path required a consignment of some 50,000 units for the test town. It featured a jolly graphic motif using lettering that resembled the product in its crisp puffy bulginess, and showed a couple of young people being wafted aloft by a bunch of crisp golden spheres.

'Savoury Nut Puffs,' ran the inscription on the front. 'The taste that takes you to the top! New!'

The pack itself was something of a novelty. Ordinary potato-crisp paper was too hydroscopic; moisture would render the product unacceptably gooey, and so they were using a new crackly-transparent plastifoil material to allow maximum protection while affording the all-important appetite-appeal of the product to shine through.

Accompanied by the marionette-mouthed Bryan, she held frequent meetings with the advertising agency who had come up with a poster campaign featuring the same balloony motif and the words 'YOU'VE GOT TO TAKE 'EM UP OR YOU'LL FEEL LET DOWN.'

A radio campaign had also been devised featuring a jingle based on the old tune, 'Pack Up Your Troubles in Your Old Kit Bag'. But they'd changed the words to 'We've packed up our bubbles in the new foil bag'.

The use of the old marching song offended her instinctively when she first heard it. They weren't to know that her father had been a soldier, and turned faces of condescending incomprehension when she remonstrated.

'Isn't that a little like mocking the dead?'

Bryan, of course, defended it with all his customary fatuity.

'People don't think of it as a soldier's song any more, you know, Charlet.'

The agency man nodded in his wake.

'It's a good fun tune,' Bryan continued, unstoppably, 'covering the widest spectrum of consumer attitudes. Kids will like it but it's not childish. It's not over-trendy. The young housewife can relate to it. And the middle-aged won't feel left out in the cold. It's a little up-market but that helps justify the higher price.'

She suddenly realized why Bryan closed his mouth so quickly after speaking. It served to keep the spit in.

'We'll reserve judgement on that one,' she said firmly, and asked the agency to go away and come up with an alternative.

The team gazed at her with thinly veiled hostility. Bryan rolled his head like a ventriloquist's dummy and fixed his eyes on the ceiling. She knew that, in their view, she was simply being obstructive, but she felt her father would have been proud of her.

'I'm a soldier's daughter,' she told them to try and melt the ice, but she knew they would merely take it as evidence of female subjectivity.

Later that day, she had a phone call from Bruce.

'Just what do you think you're playing at?' he enquired.

'No one's playing. Working rather hard actually.'

'Don't give me all that shit. That jingle you've got is good. We haven't got time to frig around with alternatives. Waste of money anyway.'

'But . . .'

'You're letting subjective criteria undermine your commercial judgement. It's playing into the hands of the anti-female lobby at Marketing Manager level.'

'I just think it's bad taste.'

'All right. Okay. So you've got a guilt thing about your father. Don't bring it to work with you.'

Charlet realized she'd made a mistake confiding in him. Hurt and angry, she hit back.

'How the hell did you come to hear about the jingle anyway?'

'Bryan played it to me.'

'He had no right to go behind my back.'

'Oh come on. You've got such a pretty little ass, you've got to be used to people going behind your back by now.'

The joke was in the wrong taste at the wrong time, but that had never worried Bruce.

'I just think it's disloyal, that's all.'

'You're being paranoid.'

There are times, she thought, when paranoia is justified. She was a Lilliputian pinned down by Gullivers. She thought of her father.

Bruce took her silence for agreement.

'Good-oh. That's settled, then. Now, what do we have on shelf-life?'

There was nothing she could do. The realization demoralized her. What was the point of it all?

'Shelf-life, Charlet?' Bruce repeated, tapping his teeth with his gold pencil.

'Oh. Yes. Kesler's handling that. Fine. I understand everything's . . .' she cast around for something that sounded positive and cogent but the cupboard was bare.

'Fine,' she repeated.

27

After the brilliant early days of Fastfoods' stardom – the expansive phase of Affleck's first successes – a sort of implosion had set in; and now, while of course paying lip-service to ideas, the great business was to ensure that nothing happened as busily as possible. It was a tendency that had been noted before. But every week that passed confirmed it.

Some said it was because Affleck's fires had burned

low. He had never been quite the same since he had contracted hepatitis on a visit to Fastfoods, Bangkok. Others mooted that he had contracted something even more ticklish.

At all events, he now glowered out at the world with a mixture of frustration and truculence on a diet of low fats and mineral water. Having been an advertising copywriter in his youth, he now, instead of making big decisions, confined himself to making changes in pack copy.

It was said that, until he retired, no one was prepared to take any real risks.

Others, more philosophical or neurotic, said that this was now the nature of large companies, or saw a conspiracy with the government in which the new efficiency was to keep inefficiency at a suitably high level, thus ensuring maximum employment for the ever-growing middle class.

At all events, a fatal malfunction had set in.

As in the body when the brain sends messages of movement to the locomotor system, but some fatal chemical or neurological disorder frustrates the passing of the message – or as in the farmyard when a mother hen suddenly for no apparent reason starts eating her chicks – so in Fastfoods had committees and subcommittees analysing qualitative and quantitative, parametric and non-parametric research negated the corporate brainbox and finally baffled its better instincts.

Occasionally, it was true, specific projects did eventually see the light of day, but these simply existed to disprove any possible criticism of company inactivity; they were mock suckers, not real shoots; and even if they had been, there were simply not enough of them to threaten anyone's patch or pose any real threat of change and progress. Thus even the positive manifestations were merely symptoms of the energetic circular activity that governed the central politics and philosophy of the place.

Certain massive early-Affleck brands formed the under-pinning of its economy. These were staple snackstuffs that had been launched in Fastfoods' heyday and had captured an inalienable hold on the market. Every other new project had to match up to these megaliths, and of course it was seen that they never did. You were never blamed for developing a product and having it researched to death at Fastfoods. The ultimate crime was to launch and then have a slow sell-out, however much ultimate potential the product might have. It had to be Big and Fast. Otherwise it simply wasn't Fastfoods.

The management of the company was like some implac-able Moloch to whom Ideas were a sort of human sacrifice. Notion after notion was fed screaming into its fiery orifice, and still it gaped and still it asked for more.

All this was known, but it was the interpretation that was put on it that differed. To most of the employees at Fastfoods, conditioned beyond commonsense, it was a challenge. They really felt it was possible to beat the system while knowing rationally that it was impossible. They moaned about it in the company cafeteria, they made scurrilous little jokes about it in Buddies Bar, but they never stopped poking about with their gap analyses trying to find holes in the tired old market.

So it was that Charlet had come to regard the Nut Puff project.

It was evidence, badly needed, that her life, though in disorder at its edges, had a central motif of promise and progress which made all the frustrations and insecurities on the way seem like a fleeting pimple (and talking of pimples, for the first time in her life she had begun to suffer from the little beasts, little white eruptions manifesting after some of her heavier nights, though she put it down to a new urea-rich seaweed-extract natural cream she was using).

She knew it was going to be like winning a lottery –

unlikely but triumphant – and she presented her plans for the launch to the Policy Committee with a pride and excitement that was painful to contain. (Could it be, after all, that she really was a Fastfoods Person?)

After she had shown them the basic concept both on chart and board, she unveiled the product itself. First she discoursed upon the pack, dwelling particularly on the pack copy, and then she distributed little individual trays for each member of the Board.

They helped themselves gravely, showing no emotion, giving no hint that they were stoking their libidos, but chewing like mastodons as she talked through the actual pack design, now printed, which made the product radiant as Jove's golden orb rather than the dusky-wafery hues of the real thing but that was what pack design was for.

The committee chewed and nodded as she handed over to the advertising agency. She knew it was not in the nature of such things for anyone to show enthusiasm at this stage, but she looked around for clues as the agency director exposed the point-of-sale material, the posters, and finally the radio commercials.

'We've packed up our bubbles in the new foil bag . . .' warbled the Presentation Room's lavish new stereo machines through huge adjusto-directional speakers now inclined towards Mr Affleck like obsequious sandwich boards.

Though she might disagree with the choice of music, she could not help being impressed with the plausibility of the whole thing. There was nothing like advertising for turning a project into a product. It made Nut Puffs really come to life.

And it seemed from the minutely registered but none-theless discernible reactions of the Committee – a scratched nose here, a lobe tugged there, small things but indicative to the trained eye – that they agreed with her.

Even Affleck appeared to be tapping his gold pencil in

time to the music, ready to get his red lead into a faultily placed full-point.

The advertising had performed its task of breaking the ice, and apart from one or two questions of product formulation, profit forecast and public relations, there were no serious hiccups in the rest of her presentation.

Indeed, her old form with all its sparkle, cheekiness, dash and confidence seemed to have returned, and she gave the performance of her life.

Bruce himself, seated next to Affleck, was in a rare mood of public cooperation, nodding and smiling encouragement.

Only Kesler at the back, a black shadow like something that crawled out of a water-butt, seemed to be impervious to the brio of her presentation. She could have killed him when Affleck, after ruminatively sucking at a bubble, shot her a question about shelf-life.

Knowing that it was good to be seen including her team in her moment of glory, she referred the question back to him.

'I think David Kesler, my uh Brand Manager here, can shed a little light on that one. David?'

'Yes.'

Typical of him to play dumb.

'The shelf-life figures.'

'I believe they are correct.'

'Yes, David. But what are they?'

'I gave them to you, I believe.'

He had indeed given them to her, pages of neatly laid-out figures, which, with her various preoccupations, she had never really had time to digest. Instead, she had merely asked Kesler if everything was in order. She remembered him assuring her at the time that the figures were absolutely watertight.

Now she felt annoyed at his unforthcomingness, and made a little joke about it.

'David is always so backward in coming forwards.'

There was a little titter at his expense, and Charlet could see his white face clouding pink. Serve him right. But now she'd have to bluff her way through any further technical questions without him. Could she afford to do this?

'Yes,' she said, modifying her position, judging that she might yet pull him back into the fold, 'he's too modest to spell it out but David's been up there in Skelmington really taking the product apart with Production. Just as Bryan . . .'

She turned and flashed a smile which left Bryan gaping like a guppy.

'. . . Just as Bryan really grafted away in Gomborough on all the pre-launch logistics. I may as well say here and now that I couldn't have got Nut Puffs off the ground without them. Either of them. The best of back-ups I could wish for.'

It was so manifestly insincere that it fooled everyone. It totally took the wind out of any sabotage that Kesler might have been planning and it left Bryan with nothing further to add.

The Committee, while not believing her for one moment, could see that her two junior colleagues were deeply stirred. She sensed them mumbling away at their decision-making processes, thinking what a good man-manager she was.

She finished on a spring tide of self-esteem.

When the advertising agency and the one or two other outsiders had left, Bruce (as Marketing Manager overseeing the project) rose to conclude the presentation.

For a moment, it was true, a chiffon of doubt wisped across her mind. He had so often behaved bleakly towards her in front of his peers to emphasize that there was nothing between them in case anyone should accuse them of complicity: not that anyone in the company should have had the slightest inkling of their liaison. No one else knew about it except Poppy, and she was her best friend. She would never let on.

And yet there had been the incident of the blurred but outrageous photograph of a couple unmistakably making love on the floor of an office which had appeared on the sixth floor noticeboard one day.

No face and indeed no detail apart from the unquestionable nature of the act in hand could be discerned, but there was something that vaguely suggested – impossible though the notion was – that it might have been herself and Bruce thrashing away on the middle management Wilton.

Naturally the thing had been removed within an hour of its appearance, but it had made Bruce relentless and publicly sardonic towards her for a week.

(Infuriating, she had thought, that the episode – if it were common knowledge – would be counted to reflect credit on Bruce and odium on her.)

There were other little incidents, or had she imagined them? Sniggering in the washroom, suddenly stifled giggles at the programmers' Insta-Snack Point, inexplicable mirth in Merchandising, which led her to think that at some recent stage their secret had been sniffed out, and at other times led her to suspect that the offender was none other than Bruce himself.

At all events, on this occasion, the suspicion raced away to the ends of the Universe because, as soon as he opened his mouth, Charlet knew that Bruce had at last come good.

'Congratulations, Charlet,' he said. 'I think that comes from all of us. It's well ordered, cogently thought out. It has, yes, the temper of decision. It feels good. Our Managing Director,' here he gave a little hand-quirk at Mr Affleck, 'asked me personally to give Charlet her head on this one. I've deliberately stood back and let her get on with it. So the credit is entirely down to her along with the responsibility. Normally, of course, I might've been tempted to stick my oar in . . .'

Here he looked over the top of his gold glasses. Charlet thought she detected the ghost of a laugh from the back. Or was it just Bryan and his eternal nose-blowing? Bruce continued.

'But no, in deference to our Managing Director's wishes, I have resolutely pulled back. So I can claim little credit for what looks to me like being a remarkably successful exercise. All that remains is for us to get a good reading from Gomborough – the decision to go for a test market first was one stipulation I did make – it was Charlet's quite understandable wish to go national straight away. But, once tested, I can see nothing but gold for Nut Puffs. And, if you will forgive me for mixing the metaphor, I forecast that they're going to be one of the brightest bubbles in the Fastfoods crown.'

He sat down. There was the nearest to applause that ever happened at Marketing Committee meetings in John Keats House.

Affleck nodded as if to endorse his words, which was a sign of the rarest favour, and after a brief exchange of notes with the Finance Director – Affleck believed in handing notes to people at public meetings, it got everyone on their toes thinking they might be being privately criticized – he withdrew, followed in pecking order by Directors, Marketing Head, Marketing Managers, Group Brand Managers, Senior Brand Managers and anything else that crawled upon the face of the earth.

Charlet walked back to the office with her team.

Even as she passed down the corridor, she sensed that somehow the word was out. There seemed a new mood of optimism in the place, a breeze of hope, a ripple of possibility. Was she imagining it, or were the nervous

139

malice and envious snickerings suddenly replaced by a natural and infectious happiness and spontaneity?

A girl was actually singing as she came out of a lift.

A single clear laugh came up the well of the stairs.

It was like the end of a long winter.

The system had been beaten.

Even Bryan and Kesler appeared to be impressed by the way things had gone, and lingered in her office, discussing the finer points of the Committee's reactions. Bryan chattered away like a typewriter.

'They seemed to like it, didn't they? You think so, David? I think so. It reminds me of a presentation I once gave to Burga-Pipe . . .'

The only thing that slightly puzzled her was why Bruce, who was never slow to do himself a good turn, had so signally played down his role in the project. She knew he had been instrumental in deciding to go ahead with it in the first place. Why had he not mentioned it? Why was there no mention of experimentation with pheromones?

But she was too happy to think about it. As Bryan rambled on in his customary manner, interposing totally unconnected and yet always fatuous parentheses into the mainstream of his monologue ('saw this gorgeous girl getting off a bus yesterday, incidentally how do you spell fulfil?'), her thoughts drifted away beyond the moment into a delicious area of reverie where strange shapes and images nibbled like goldfish at the fringes of her consciousness.

28

She needed to go home. She was out of clothes. Besides, she felt her sense of promise and breakthrough was big enough now to encompass both sides of her existence.

When she arrived home, she didn't head for the dubious welcome of the kitchen where rubber chimaera or bouncy boa constrictor might have upset her mood of elation. Instead she went straight upstairs to her little office cum workroom. But the monsters had extended their range. The room was crammed with Pentelle's patterns – fangs, claws, warts, whiskers, predatory beaks and scaley legs dripped and slithered over every conceivable surface. It was like some ghastly paper charnel house.

But even that didn't get her down.

She was so tired, felt so complete in herself, that she made no fuss, felt none of that familiar surge of exasperation and distance, simply went to the spare bedroom, took off her clothes, got into bed and turned off the light.

She lay there for a little, hearing laughter and shouts from the other end of the house, and toyed with the idea of going down and saying hullo, but fell into a delicious and headlong sleep before she could summon the will.

At an indefinite midnight hour, something woke her. And for some reason her immediate instinct was not to move or in any way let on that she was awake.

Opening her eyes imperceptibly, she saw in the weak glimmer of the street lamp, Howard sitting on the bed looking down at her.

Oh God, she thought, not something jelly-like and bouncy, not something hairy with tubes in it, not a scuttling clockwork tarantula. She braced herself for the inevitable jape, still sensing however that if she wasn't seen to be awake, he might just go away.

He gazed down. She peered up. Still nothing happened. No troll, no skeleton, no spindly thing with chattering teeth, no slime, no leprous jelly. It was unprecedented.

She began to feel familiar sensations of irritation. She valued her sleep and if someone was going to come along and wake her up after a hard day, he'd better have a good reason and not sit there mooning like a yoghurt.

But as he turned his head very slightly towards the light, she noticed an unfamiliar glimmer on his face, and realized that he was weeping.

He was normally so quiet, so contained, that this was a considerable revelation. Did he come up and weep over her often when she was asleep? (She had taken to using the spare room now on her trips home.)

She felt a quirk of guilt. Then she felt annoyed again. What should she do? Could she not escape decisions even in the night? Should she now pretend to wake up and comfort him? Or should she just feign sleep and hope he'd go away?

He made no sound. The tears seemed crystallized upon his cheeks like retsina tappings.

She closed her eyes, her eyelids sinking with the feathery softness of a fern, and lay breathing regularly until at last she felt him get up and pad away down the corridor.

In the morning she almost felt that she might have dreamt the whole thing. He made no reference to it as she snatched a quick cup of coffee.

'Sorry I snuck in like that last night,' she said. 'I was knackered. You know how it is.'

'I know how it is,' he said.

She almost asked him if he'd been in her room last night but she felt he might read things into it that she didn't mean.

142

'How are the monsters?' she asked instead. 'Never seen so many monsters in a place. Hell must feel positively underpopulated.'

'We've had to commandeer your workroom, I'm afraid. Can't keep up with the orders.'

'Oh,' she said, pretending that she didn't know.

'We have to have a place for the patterns. Pentelle's working like a black Trojan beaver.'

'Just ask her to let me have it back when she's finished with it, would you?'

She didn't see why she should have to let the mousy creature run roughshod all over her, even if she was a visitor in her own home.

Though some of yesterday's good humour remained, there was a certain briskness in her this morning.

'Oh, I will. When she's finished with it.'

There was a silence.

'Charlet,' he said suddenly.

She paused on her way out.

'What?'

Was he going to spill the beans after all? Tell her how much he loved, how much he missed her? But he just stood there slowly turning his head from side to side.

'What is it?' she asked. 'I'm in rather a rush actually.'

'What d'you think of them?'

For the first time, she took a close look at him. It was not her practice to peer at people over breakfast.

'My God,' she said.

He was wearing, on either side of his nose, great tear-shaped plastic stick-on things with little snouts and legs.

'What are they?'

'Crocodile tears,' he said. 'We've an order for 25,000. You could stop work if you want to now.'

'You must be joking,' she said.

143

29

Later, at work that morning, she had a sudden twinge not actually of guilt but of guilt about not feeling guilt about the children. She really ought to take more interest.

She realized, of course, that they weren't particularly interested in her, but all the same they were only little squirts where she was a grown person. The ball was in her court. She knew it was their half-term, so she called home. Her son answered.

'Ear,' he said, 'Eye nose you.'

It was the name of Howard's new company.

'Hullo. It's me.'

'Oh, hullo Group Brand Mummager. Mummagin all right?'

There was something horribly condescending about him, as opposed to his sister who was merely chilly.

'Fine, thank you,' she said. 'And you?'

'I'm a bit tied up at the moment, actually. Could you come to the point?'

'I wondered if you'd like to come to the cinema with me this evening.'

She mentioned a film which she'd heard them talking about.

'Well . . .' the boy considered the suggestion. 'We're a bit tied up at the moment.'

He sounded more and more like a Fastfoods Senior Research Executive. She began to lose patience.

'I've got tickets. Get your father to bring you. I could run you all back in the Pork.'

She used the children's irreverent name for her car.

'But . . .'

'No buts. You're not a goat.'

It was a poor joke but there wasn't the ghost of a laugh.

'This is all most irregular,' the child said.

'See you there at seven.'

She put the phone down before he could say anything more.

She hadn't in fact got any tickets, although she'd established they were available. She needn't have bothered even to do that, as it happened.

The children didn't turn up.

30

The circular tendency in large companies like Fastfoods was well exemplified by the activity surrounding the registration of brand names.

Company lawyers always liked the nice warm feeling of being able to wave a piece of paper at any competitor who came along with a similarly named product, proving that their company had an inalienable right to it.

Although it was not strictly necessary – you could always sue for imitation or 'passing off' – it was much less complicated and expensive in the event of litigation to have the whole thing nicely sewn up with the Registrar.

It was perfectly understandable. It was also vastly profitable to the lawyers, the various ramifications of the Registrar's Office, and the cloud of agents which hummed about it.

But the result was that every conceivable name under the sun had already been registered by some company or other.

Computer runs as well as human brains had exhausted

(one would think) every outlandish variant of syllable, and still they poured out into the memory banks.

Of course, it did not mean that the actual product was similarly protected. The Patent's Office saw to that. You could only patent a product if it included some original process, which inevitably most food products didn't.

Marketing theory tended to deride originality anyway. It was too risky, required too much investment. There were times, of course, when it was inevitable but the general practice was to do a 'me-too' – that was, to copy someone else's product and re-package it. And give it a new name.

The result was the growth of the Name Industry.

Charlet had known about the name-game long before. She had always accepted it as part of the obstacle course that made life at Fastfoods so fascinating as well as so frustrating – so fascinating because it *was* so frustrating – but as she sat looking at the print-out of names that the company had already on register, she was aware of a familiar surge of thwarted bafflement. Why were they showing her these tortured syllables?

She summoned her two Brand Managers.

'For Christ's sake, Bryan,' she said, 'I thought we had the name Nut Puffs registered. What the hell's all this? We're launching in three weeks' time. The packs are printed. The posters are in production. What's going on in this place?'

'A new directive, Charlet, actually. Nut Puffs was apparently not registerable as it consists of everyday English words. I assume the decision was taken to go ahead and simply trade with the name since no one else is using it. But a memo's just come in from the legal department reminding us of company policy. So I thought we'd get the computer to cough up a few alternatives.'

He looked at her with ridiculous joy, all enthusiasm and no sense.

Charlet felt a lurch of apprehension. Was this some responsibility of the pilot group under Bruce that had spawned the project which they had shelved and passed on to her? She had had every reason to believe when she took the thing on that the naming of the product had been approved way back. All the same, she had not looked into it. The responsibility was now hers.

She glanced again at the gibberish list in front of her.

PUFFETS
PUFFETTES
PUFFLETS
PUFFLETTES
PUFFEX
PUFF-X
PUFFESS
PUFNUTS
PUFNUFS
PUFSNUF

There were thirty or more variants on PUF. Then the machine had gone to work on NUT.

NUTPUF
NUTPUC
NUTFUP
NUTFUC

She glanced up at Bryan, who was watching her with an expression of loony concern, and across at Kesler, who was scarcely concealing a smirk of satisfaction. All the bonhomie and promise of the previous evening had been simply a snare and delusion, merely the grass over the tiger-trap. She had the strongest suspicion that Kesler had known about this all along.

Her aptitude for nausea came to her aid. She had to leave the room fast but she was going to settle this before she went.

'Knowing Legal, there's no guarantee that they've done an update on the availability of these names. We simply don't have time to piss around. We're going with Nut Puffs.'

Bryan opened his mouth very wide and spoke very fast.

'WedidhavearatherunfortunateexperienceatTasti-Meal . . .'

'Fuck Tasti-Meal. Indeed Nutfuc Tasti-Meal.'

Bryan's mouth dropped shut like a portcullis, giving the impression that he was still talking inside, the syllables scrabbling at his teeth like fugitive soldiery trying to get out.

'I'm leaving the office now,' said Charlet. 'I have to go and see the below-the-line people.'

'I saw them yesterday,' said Kesler.

'For crying out loud,' she said. 'I'm going to see the below-the-line people. All right?'

'All right,' they replied in unison.

'And don't go and winge to Bruce.'

'All right,' they said again.

She knew they lied.

Luddington was sucking a lozenge in the lift. He offered her one.

'No thanks,' she said. 'I'm in a bit of a panic, got to rush.'

'Panic,' he mused. 'Now there's a word. You know that Lud's equated by some with Pan? If you're feeling panic, what you're really feeling could be Lud-ic. Oh, he's stirring all right. Never you fear for that.'

Outside the building, she drew a deep breath. The air was grey with the smoke of passing traffic but it tasted good after the filtered anonymity, tinged with Bryan's after-shave, of the office.

Sensing that she was being monitored at a discreet distance by Kesler, she made a circuit of the building, dodged behind a truck, snicked down a side alley, and made for Buddies Bar, confident it would be empty of Fastfoods people at this hour.

After a couple of brandies, she felt better but she couldn't bring herself to go back just yet. Why should she, after all? She had earned a break. It was still early – just after eleven. Why shouldn't she get in her car (locking the doors from the inside this time), drive down to the Old City, and look up that last address they'd given her for her father?

It was something she'd been meaning to do, and what was more it'd show Bruce and Co that she wasn't a neurotic panicker who was going to wet herself every time the Company Lawyer wagged his finger.

As she collected the Porsche from the garage and drove through the familiar centre of the city eastwards, she played absurd romantic games in her head about finding her father, nursing him, providing in the few years left to him that his broken health allowed, the homely comforts that he had never known.

Even as the options drifted across her mind, she realized that this was most unlike her. Families were not her strong point. What sort of mother had she been to her children? But then, wasn't it because of the absence of family life in her case that she felt so little for Howard and the children? Her emotions had had no potty training in that direction.

Perhaps once she had found her father, she might discover that centre in herself which would allow the softer qualities to show themselves. At the moment, she could not show what she did not feel.

She drove on. The offices and shops, showrooms and hotels, the great buildings of the banks and the financial institutions, the cathedrals of God and Mammon, slowly gave way to other more dowdy replicas of John Keats sticking up out of areas of little dwellings like beeheemoths.

At last she came to a network of gaunt blackened broken-windowed warehouses and deserted tenements punctuated by abandoned churches which ran in unbroken dereliction beside the river.

Some of these streets were already being razed to make way for the new River City which an over-optimistic Housing Minister had proclaimed before losing office, but which no successor had had the courage to cancel. Indeed Charlet, consulting her street guide, was afraid that Sophia Street had already fallen under the bulldozer. But on closer inspection the huge puffing buffaloes and siege engines, glimpsed between cracks in a palisade, still seemed mercifully distant from the place where she understood it to be. She stopped and asked a ramshackle old woman standing beside a strip of wilderness.

'Sophia Street? Well d'you know, I knows it, but all at once I seems not to have it. I daresay . . . I daresay . . .' she said, looming closer and fixing Charlet with a meaning eye, 'I daresay a little something would refresh me memory.'

Charlet gave her money.

'Thank you, dear,' said the old girl, 'I was born down these parts. Now it's like the end of the world. It *is* the end of the world. Sophia Street's the next one along. Named after an Empress, it was. Not that she ever came down.'

Charlet thanked her.

'Not at all, my dear. Any time. Come again, any time you like. I'll be 'ere. Bless you, my lady. End of the fucking world. Look out for them foxes, though. Like bleeding dogs they are round 'ere.'

It was, when she arrived, quite a handsome street. Even now – paneless, boarded up, sagging-roofed, with weeds fuzzing like unwanted hair from lintel and guttering

– the classical proportions of the four-storey buildings lent an air of distinction to the general ruin.

Each house had a big crude numeral splashed in white paint across its boards or door, presumably in anticipation of demolition. The address she'd been given for her father was Number 47. She drove slowly past, noting that it appeared perhaps marginally better preserved than some of its neighbours. It at least had its door on.

Then she swung the car round at the next junction and parked by the curve in the street so that she could both observe and, if necessary, escape.

She checked again the locks on both doors, wound up the windows, and gazed out at the unpromising scene before her.

There was no sign of human life in the street whatever. An old black one-eared tomcat padded up the pavement sniffing hopelessly at the litter. Smoke from the distant demolition works drifted across the lower end of the street giving it a foretaste of eclipse. A broken shutter flapped. A small indeterminate machine whined and dithered in the distance.

She had waited for twenty minutes or so, and was about to abandon observation in favour of a more frontal approach like, say, a knock on the front door (the place was so lowered it had had the effect of bolstering her courage) when she was aware of movement in the building opposite Number 47.

There was a sort of bulging of the corrugated iron sheet which served as its front door, and a shuffling figure sidled out dressed in some sort of shapeless raincoat done up with string, carrying two pieces of wood and a grimy sack. Without looking to left or right, it made for the basement stairs of the house across the street, throwing the wood down over the side as it went.

In normal circumstances, such an event would not have been surprising in any run-down part of town. There was now a substantial unofficial population of ragamuffins, vagabonds, vagrants and hobbledehoys in the areas which were officially designated as depopulated. But there was something odd about this particular figure. His raggedy brown coat, his walk, that grizzled head . . . it was the very tramp who had been dogging her for the past few months.

Suddenly her mind was full of possibilities. Perhaps he had not been a threat after all. Perhaps he had been trying in his poor crazed way to communicate with her. He knew who she was. And now it began to seem to her that she knew who he was too. Why else would he be here in this god-and-man forsaken place, other than to cling to the wreckage of his old life. It could be. It should be him. The coincidences were too far-fetched to hint at anything other than the truth.

Her first instinct was to run over to the house, beat at the door, and throw herself into his arms. But there was still a shadow of doubt in her mind. The moment didn't seem right. She felt she needed to be absolutely ready for this moment of rediscovery. It would come. She knew where he was now. Certain things had to be settled, disposed of, first.

She started the car and drove back to John Keats House.

In her office, the telephone was ringing. It was Bruce in his most cutting form.

'Where the hell have you been?'

'Out.'

'Evidently. But on what score?'

'I needed to check on something.'

'I see. I rather wondered whether you hadn't gone for an interview. Looking for another job might have been rather wise under the circumstances.'

In spite of her new-found fund of certainty, Charlet

felt a needle of panic. Finding a father was one thing, but now she needed money more than ever.

It wasn't so easy to get jobs at the moment, and Bruce knew it.

'It was a personal matter, Bruce.'

'Ah. Seeing your gynaecologist, no doubt. I don't know, you women in business. You treat your bodies like a pacifist treats his conscience. An excuse for not doing anything that might be a bit too much like hard work. Vivat vagina.'

The remark was deliberately offensive at just about every level, particularly from a man who had so singularly enjoyed the benefits of that organ. Charlet was incensed.

'Would you mind repeating that? I have a tape-recorder here. I'm sure Personnel would be most interested in your . . .'

'Fuck the tape-recorder. What're you going to do about the name?'

'Nothing at all. We're going to go with Nut Puffs.'

'Even though it may cost us a million?'

'Even though.'

'You'd better come and explain it to Mr Affleck. I'm afraid he's not quite as confident as you are.'

'Why wasn't all this settled before I took over?'

'You were given responsibility for the whole project, Charlet. Not just part of it. All of it. If you feel you're not up to shouldering a Senior Group Brand Managership you only have to say. From where I'm sitting, it's beginning to look as if our confidence in you was misplaced.'

'Where are you sitting?'

'The Managing Director's office. You'd better come over right away.'

Almost weeping with mortification and that fear whose whiff permeates executive corridors, she trailed up to the seventeenth floor by the stairs. Although there was always the chance that you might get one of the other lifts, she couldn't face the though of Luddington. He had become oppressively familiar recently, as if at any moment he would ask her to be his thurifer.

Affleck was brittle to the point of fracture.

'Well?' he snapped.

'There's no time to change the name, I'm afraid.'

'Whose fault is that?'

'Well . . .?'

She glanced at Bruce but there was no help from that quarter. Affleck rapped on his desk with the gold-plated ballpoint from the inkstand in the shape of a vintage Rolls that the car-leasing company had given him for Christmas.

'Are you in charge of the launch of Nut Puffs?' he asked.

'Yes but . . .'

'Yes or no?'

'Yes.'

'That is all there is to it. I agree with you. It is too late to change the name. There is now only one other question. Do we abort the whole project in light of the risk we run from possible competition or litigation? Or do we launch?'

'We stand to lose our whole investment so far if we stop now,' she said.

'I also agree. That is why we shall go ahead at this stage. Bruce?'

She would not only never see him again if he failed to back her up now. She would have Luddington throw him down the lift-shaft.

Bruce hesitated. And then finally nodded.

'Yes,' he said, 'I think we've got to go with this one.'

'But,' cautioned Affleck, shaking his pencil at Charlet, 'and it's a very big but, if there's any comeback, any claim from anyone with a whiff of a chance of a passing-off action, you know who I'll be gunning for, don't you?'

'And that means you, Charlet,' said Bruce unnecessarily.

Charlet nodded. Being good in bed and horrible in public was better than the reverse, but not much.

She felt caught up in an action the outcome of which, whatever it was, had already been decided.

She closed the door heavily behind her and walked back down the corridor. Feeling dizzy for a moment, she leaned against the wall, then realized that Luddington was beckoning to her hieratically from round the corner. She roused herself and followed him. He had his lift waiting like a coach.

'Enter,' he said, elaborately, doffing his cap and bowing, 'princess.'

She could not very well refuse.

'I want you to come down to my cubby-hole,' he told her. 'There's things in there that no one's seen. Lud things. You will be startled.'

'I'd love to,' she said, 'but I'm rather busy at the moment.'

'Lud can wait,' said Luddington, 'but can you wait for him? If you ask me you need help. I know what's going on round these parts. They think I'm nutty but if you ask me the boot's on the other foot.'

31

Bamstead was spreading car jokes about her if the latest graffiti in the tenth floor cloakroom were anything to go by; Poppy seemed to be behaving like a groupie, screwing in less than three months more men than Charlet had managed in as many years; another of those photographs had appeared on the fifth floor noticeboard, and had as quickly been taken down again. But none of these things seemed now of the slightest consequence.

Only two issues dominated her life.

On the mundane side, she had to concentrate on the imminent Nut Puffs launch. The name panic apart, the news was good. The Sales people had reported an excellent sell-in. A 'teaser' campaign of posters was already going up featuring immense golden speech bubbles and ingratiating little jokes: 'Gomborough, we're nuts about you,' and 'A bubble's in trouble if it's not in Gomborough.' Considerable consumer interest had been generated, and the public relations people were haring around preparing for the opening of a local crèche for the children of working mothers named after the product itself: The Nut Puff Nursery.

Charlet gave interviews to the Trade Press, had her photograph taken for the Fastfoods House Magazine, *Fastlane*, approved the final tapes for the radio campaign, and even appeared in Gomborough for a pre-launch whistle-stop jamboree to put the love of Mammon into any dithering dealers.

Her father, or at least the possibility of his existence, dominated everything, satisfying her emotions even if he could not always fill her thoughts. She was saving him up for afterwards.

As her days grew longer, she made more and more use of the Waiting Room, only going home to collect fresh clothes. She had moved all her things there up to the attic. She knew Pentelle was afraid of heights.

It was warm up there. She sometimes used to sit like a child, knees hunched up to her face, hands fondling the old letters, her face rapt, her mind floating on benign currents.

She had in her heart known that she would never find anyone who felt the foreign-ness of life the way she did. But now the prospect of a father, the missing half of her life who would understand and warm the chilly cockles of her alone-ness, imbued her with a kind of restless impatience.

She could feel the unused part of her filling and warming, opening like parched roots to rain, while the superficial Charlet became more and more an appendage, a superfluous thumb, an appendix whose purpose might have had past relevance but had no practical application now.

She spoke to few people in these later days. The official business was over. Even the meetings had petered out.

Later, of course, there would be sales analyses to be examined, research results, consumer reaction panels, discussion groups – and finally the gearing-up of the local activity to a national fold-out.

But now, after all the preparation, there was suddenly nothing left to do, nothing to say.

She came into the office late, stayed long over lunch which she ate by herself in a gloomy cellar which was really a nightclub but opened for the extra little bit of lunchtime trade. No one from Fastfoods ever came there. It was too far for the average executive to walk, not smart enough to be worth riding to.

At her desk she declined invitations to coffee, doodled on her blotter, and ignored her two Brand Managers who – although they were not by nature likely to be buddies – united against her in a quite overt display of indifference.

She had noticed before, an incidence of earnestness among most of the younger Brand Managers. Although Fastfoods was supposed to be in the lighter bubblier side of the food business, it was not the done thing to be joyful. A smile indicated loose thinking.

Every now and then, when they thought she wasn't listening, she could hear Kesler and Bryan exchanging sounds which not merely appeared to be robbed of all meaning but seemed to be totally devoid of emotion.

157

'I don't think we should heavy this one, David.'

'No, Bryan. You are right. It needs finessing.'

'What about the Bruce-Charlet axis?'

'I think that's just kiddology, frankly.'

'You mean in the final analysis it . . .'

'You're an intelligent person, Bryan. I'd be defaulting in my duty if I . . .'

There was a mutter of something that Charlet could not quite catch.

'You don't suppose they'll have a rethink? You know, devolve the whole thing to a more general basis?'

'No, Bryan. We're well skewed-out on this one. I've minuted every sequence.'

Charlet knew they were hatching something grey and foul, but they couldn't reach her now.

And so back to Bruce, always back to Bruce, neither of them giving anything away, attracted by mutual dislike; out of sight of the office, he still behaved towards her with exemplary consideration. He took her to the best restaurants, filling her like a Strasbourg goose with the choicest delicacies before providing the quietus, in the privacy of the Waiting Room, with a cruelly and wonderfully prolonged bare bodkin.

She knew, of course, that it would have to stop when her father came to stay, she wanted it to; but, until the appointed time, she accepted the nightly sentence, concurred in it, twitched, gibbered and danced to it with all the more relish because it was so soon to end.

Her mind these days seemed like a kite which her body, that had held it tight through all its dips, wafts and curvetings, had suddenly let go. It was soaring unconstrainedly on billowing winds.

It had skewed out on this one.

32

Like a squall whose approach across hitherto calm water is easy to chart; the rushing ripply shadow zigzagging on its way, the fretful wavelets, the other boats heeling over in the blast; but the force of whose arrival is nonetheless unforeseeably shocking; so the great day of the Gomborough launch arrived with a sickening lurch.

She had travelled up with Bruce, David and Bryan the day before to stay in the Gamecock Motel and Conference Centre.

After an eerie dinner in the Cockpit Room at which Kesler had silently sipped mineral water and Bryan had grown drunk and garrulous, his mouth falling about like a tipsy Cossack dancer, Bruce and Charlet had said a prim public goodnight to each other, before sneaking back to her room and making love as if Berlin were about to fall.

'Junk sex,' she thought, lying afterwards on damp sheets, sipping a brandy from the mini-bar, having ticked her breakfast needs – so delicious in description, so plastic in event – and given them to the departing Bruce to hang on the doorknob as he went out.

'Gomborough,' she thought. 'Sod 'em.'

And she fell into a deep but pulse-pounding sleep, waking up in confusion at five next morning.

What was it, where was she? Ah yes, Gomborough.

Suddenly she was overwhelmed with panic. Where was Luddington now? He had spoken to her about giving her an amulet against it. Too late. Oh, she had anticipated the day well enough, but prospect never does justice to

159

physical sensation. Her head ached, her palms clammed, and her stomach felt full of puffed bolts.

Suppose nobody bought the wretched things.

She was all at once painfully aware of the sheer physical instability of her life.

No home but an attic, her job depending on a bubble, her father no more than a shadow, her only certainty the Waiting Room . . .

Waiting for what? Brucey baby.

She got up and looked at her face in the bathroom mirror under the cruel light hotel fitters rejoice to select for the passing stranger. Every spot, every crow's-foot, every bald patch thrown into stark relief. Not that she had the bald patch yet, but the lines were there at eye and mouth, like cracks in a picture.

How her enemies in the corridors of John Keats would gloat if they could see her now! The mirror even seemed to hint at unpleasant breath.

She brushed her teeth, took a shower, put on a face and dressed. Dropping a sad-looking bag of tea from the Courtesy Pack into a cup, she made a beverage which tasted of damp felt.

It was now past six o'clock. Time to switch on to the local radio station.

'Cryogenic baby, kiss me, squeeze me, freeze me,' warbled the bleak little bedhead fascia panel.

The song ended. Another voice shouldered the burden.

'Well, that's the shape of things to hum, pop-pickers, and now let's . . . take a breaaaaaaak.'

A commercial for a local builder's merchants followed, then a cute little number for a Wonder Whip, and then, glory of glories, the familiar strains that had kept those feet marching up to Passchendaele, Arras, Ypres and Hill 42.

'We've packed up our bubbles in the new foil bag . . .'

It had been given a contemporary pop arrangement, of

160

course, and it really was rather rousing in spite of all those dead soldiers. Her spirits rose. What was she worrying about? The commercial had a life, a conviction that couldn't help making an impact with all the taste-starved snack-eaters of the burg. Rum-ti-tum. She found she was tapping along in time to the perky martial strain.

She brought her breakfast tray inside, drank her orange juice, and tried to open the window so she could feed the lumpen croissant to a blackbird on the grass outside. She gave up, knowing that even if she'd managed it, the bird would have had more sense than to eat it.

It was time to meet the others.

Seeing them standing there in the plastic-rustic of the Gamecock vestibule, she could tell from a distance that a new mood had animated her dinner companions of the previous night.

'It's going to be a flier,' enthused Bryan, his teeth still piebald with quasi-croissant.

'There is a certain catchiness in the commercial,' agreed Kesler in a rare burst of concurrence.

'Early days, early days,' said Bruce, regulating and monitoring, 'but there are grounds for a modest optimism.'

They all looked at Charlet. She searched for something definitive to add. Mere agreement would be menial.

'Good aromatics,' she said.

It passed into marketingese.

There followed a tour of supermarkets and snack counters throughout the town. The thrill of seeing the first packets of Savoury Nut Puffs actually being purchased and, ultimate joy, consumed – hardened though she was to launches – was still something that came as a revelation. And then there were the favourable comments of the shopkeepers . . . and the satisfied mumbles of the consumers ('It's taste shattering,' said one woman as though she were actually in a commercial) . . . and the coverage of the event by many more of the trade papers than she had ever expected . . . and even an interview with the local TV station . . . it all indicated a quite exceptional consumer off-take even by the standards of the volatile snack market.

By the end of the day, after a reception in which the Mayor of Gomborough invited her to swing on his chain of office any time she liked, and the head of the local TV station suggested she should speak to him later about joining his staff, Charlet was exhausted but triumphant.

At dinner, they ordered champagne, and everyone except Kesler got plastered.

'Lovely bubbly,' clicked Bryan. 'It's taste-shatteringly good.'

'We must use that line in our national launch,' said Bruce. 'Well done, Bryan.'

It had been nothing to do with Bryan, thought Charlet, but she let it pass. This indirect confirmation that Bruce intended to make Nut Puffs a national brand was the culmination of her day's success.

Strangely enough, it gave her confidence in another direction. For when Bruce leant across when the others weren't looking, made a private and obscene gesture, and whispered throatily: 'Come to bed . . . I want to do this and this . . .' she suddenly found the strength to kick the habit.

'Not tonight,' she joked, though she knew he would be seriously mortified. 'I think I've puffed enough nuts for one day.'

33

Charlet was the flavour of the month once more.

The telephone started to ring again. Up-and-coming Group Brand Managers pressed her to come out to lunch. Affleck's secretary came by with an invitation to join him for a drink in the Directors' Suite. The murmur in the corridors did not stop as she passed, but became inflected with admiration. She even started to bump into Poppy, whose profile had been of late strangely submerged, on her way up from the carpark.

With the inconstancy that was a regrettable and unexcisable part of her nature, she suddenly found again that the bubble meant more to her than anything else.

Her silly obsession with her dead father, her fears of the future, everything was submerged under this new tickle coating of confidence and success. Making wheels turn, selling things to people, getting a bigger margin, scoring off the competition, these were the things that mattered. She would be Businesswoman of the Year. She would be the company's first woman Managing Director. She would found colleges, take up politics . . . All the anxiety, insecurity and frustration of the past months floated away like flavour-spray.

The word from Gomborough was nothing but good. Nut Puffs were a virtual sell-out. The only problem was getting enough product on to the shelves.

As for Bruce, she hoped he'd taken the hint at the Gamecock, and wouldn't try to undermine her resolve. However much she'd altered her opinion about what she wanted, she hadn't changed her mind about him. Luckily he'd been away on another of his overseas visitations.

However, as she sat in her office today, she noticed with a little twitch of foreboding his familiar shadow passing the other side of the frosted glass.

She prepared herself staunchly to turn down his coaxing. Those steel-rimmed headlamps could throw miraculously persuasive pools of inveiglement.

So, as soon as he strode in, she told him.

'No, Bruce.'

He blinked, affecting not to understand, waving a company carrier bag that for some reason he had with him.

'I'm sorry?'

'I said no. It's finished.'

He appeared surprised, but not quite in the way she had expected.

'Oh? So you know then?' he asked.

'Of course I know.'

'You appear to be taking it very calmly.'

'How should I take it? Histrionics? Lamentations? Seven Sobs of a Sorrowful Soul?'

'I would have expected a more responsible attitude.'

She wasn't surprised by his officious manner. She would have expected him to draw up his battle lines.

'A more responsible attitude? That's crap, Bruce, and you know it. I just don't want to sleep with you again. I don't need you, Bruce.'

'Sleep with . . . My God, woman, do you mean to say you're talking about sex?'

He said it as if she might have been speaking of woodlice.

'Well . . . yes . . .'

'You mean to say you haven't heard?'

A clammy hand gathered inside her stomach and squeezed her like a bagpipe.

'Heard? Heard what?'

'The Nut Puffs.'

164

He seemed so moved he could barely speak.

'What about the Nut Puffs?'

'There are no Nut Puffs.'

'What? What d'you mean, no Nut Puffs?

'They're bursting.'

'Nut Puffs? I don't believe it.'

He produced the familiar packet from his carrier bag, opened it and shook it out on her desk. A fine brown powder spread across the imitation tooled-leather.

'The very few packs that didn't sell out immediately must've been pushed to the back when the new delivery came. They had a week or so to wait until they reached the front. And when they were finally opened . . . they were like this. Burst, finito, kaput, exploded.'

She gazed at the powder in front of her.

'This is Nut Puffs?'

She wet her finger, dipped it gingerly in the little mound, and licked it. The flavour was unmistakable.

'Shelf-life, Charlet. I did warn you. When they vacuum-pack the bags it puts more strain on the crispy crunchy integument. I'm afraid that's down to you.'

'My God.'

Charlet sank forward on her desk, her face in her hands. The unthinkable had happened. Then suddenly she thought of something.

'But, wait a minute,' she said, clutching at straws. 'Kesler was looking after that side of things.'

'He says he sent you a memo urging extreme caution on that front. He has a copy.'

No doubt he had. Kesler had stitched her up nicely, the little toad.

'What about the people at the factory?'

'Freddie says he tried to show you an example of possible instability but you simply ignored him. Skelmington did their best, but you rushed them with the area-launch of yours. Remember I counselled caution.'

Now she recalled the label at the factory saying 'Query Fatique?'

'I was feeling sick,' she said.

It was like being back at school again. Sickness was the last excuse at the bottom of the satchel.

It hadn't worked at school, and it didn't work with Bruce either.

'You should feel sicker now. Thank God I stopped you going national.'

She did feel very sick. But even in her misery, she had the feeling that Bruce was enjoying the situation, relishing her discomfort, rubbing himself on the flanks of her misfortune. There was something evil, devilish about it. She thought of something else.

'What happened to that pheromone additive Freddie was talking about? Why wasn't I told? I can't be responsible when things have been kept from me.'

Bruce looked blank.

'Pheromone?'

'You know.'

'I'm afraid I don't know. Explain.'

'Aromatics of sexual response.'

But Bruce was not having any.

'You seem to be obsessed with sex, Charlet. Pity you can't work up some enthusiasm for your job.'

Her first instinct now was that it wasn't just Kesler who had stitched her up, it was Bruce himself. Perhaps it was simply that he'd started the project, come up against a problem and needed a scapegoat to take the blame. It was rumoured that he was a candidate for next Managing Director, he had said as much to Charlet herself. He couldn't afford to get egg on his face, so he'd flipped it on to hers.

She remembered all those times when he'd made it clear both privately and publicly that she alone was in control of the project. She recalled how often he'd stressed that he was the one to insist on a purely local try-out.

Or perhaps the place was simply possessed by a devil, and old Luddington had been right all along. Great Pan was alive and well.

At any event, she seemed to have been betrayed right across the board. And Bruce's last betrayal was not to have been even one zillionth of the strong man he pretended to be.

Her next instinct was one of panic more profound than anything she had known before, something to go right off the Lud register.

She turned back to Bruce.

'Look, Bruce, I . . .'

'Save it, Charlet.'

'We've been through a lot together.'

'Save it.'

'Please.'

'I'm going.'

'Please. Can't you . . .'

She was weeping now, although she knew it was worse than useless, and certain to give him pleasure.

'There's nothing I can do. I suggest you go home now and wait until you hear from us. It won't be immediately. We have rather a lot of pieces to pick up on this one. Lot of shit on the fan . . .'

'Please . . . I . . .'

She was actually kneeling her way across the floor like a wronged mistress – which indeed she was – tears streaming down her face, clutching at his legs. It was worth a try.

'Take me now. You want me. I know you do. Here . . . look . . .'

She pulled up her skirt, showing herself in a way that had driven him mad with desire before. He pushed her away roughly. A goggle-eyed secretary with a sheaf of

167

papers opened the door and peered in, taking in the whole scene.

Charlet knew she was finished at Fastfoods. She stood up.

'Fuck you,' she said, simply.

'No,' he replied calmly, taking off his glasses and polishing them, 'it was I who fucked you. That was one of the more taxing parts of the . . .'

He stopped himself. Charlet was convinced that he had been going to say 'job'. But how could sleeping with her be part of anything other than sleeping with her?

'But I think we can say,' he continued, pausing for a moment to replace his spectacles, 'that I discharged my duty. Congratulate me. I'm going to take over from Affleck next month.'

Charlet pushed past him and, for an instant, saw the fear in his eyes as he flinched, thinking that she would strike him, and then she was out in the corridor.

It was full now of junior Assistant Brand Managers, programmers, researchers and secretaries, stirring and rustling like carrion birds at the smell of blood.

She rolled up her sleeve and thrust out a bare arm at them.

'There you are,' she said. 'Snack. Eat.'

They shrank back, just a little, their faces witlessly malevolent.

She hurried on down the corridor, past Luddington beckoning and nodding at the door of the lift, sensing that they were following her. She started to run.

The backstairs were uncarpeted and always smelt slightly of urine and disinfectant – though who urinated upon them was a mystery since there was no access for the pissing public.

But they led down directly to the carpark, and today she wasn't fussy about the niceties, indeed she would have settled for a soiled-laundry chute.

She went down them like a chamois, scrabbling in her bag for her car-keys,

On each floor, there seemed to be more people waiting to join the pursuit: messengers, tea-ladies, catering staff, personnel manageresses with predatory glasses and shrunken skull necklaces, packaging designers, maintenance men. They all joined the mêlée, and followed her down at an ever-less-respectful distance as she slipped and stumbled on the flying concrete.

At last she was at the basement, fourteen floors down, and she burst through the door and ran across the glistening puddles where Fudgeon had been washing Affleck's Bentley.

Where had she parked the Porsche? Yes, there it was, under the pipes in the corner. She ran for it, slipped, half-fell, soaked her skirt in an oily pool, and at last she was there, trying desperately to fit the key into the lock.

As she did so, the door from the backstairs burst open and a great tide of people surged forwards: some hopping, some crawling like maggots, with clicking claws and prehensile snouts. But now she was in the car and locking the doors as they reached her. They jostled against the metal, pressing faces against the windscreen, leaving trails of slime on the glass.

Desperately she started the engine with a great roar, engaged the gear and accelerated. Nothing happened.

She realized that they had picked up the car and were rocking it, trying to turn it over.

It was heavier than they realized. They must have put it down for a second because it suddenly leapt forward in a tangle of limbs and blood, charging and scattering, pinning and ripping, until she was out, up the ramp and away, with a ripped-off arm thumping on her windscreen like a broken wiper.

She woke up. The arm was her own, thumping on the bedhead of the Waiting Room. She remembered she had gone there after the conversation with Bruce. She had finished a bottle of vodka.

She regretted that she had woken up. Reality was worse than anything.

34

The day passed slowly.

She had forgotten how dark the Waiting Room could be when the sun moved round in the later morning.

She opened a bottle of wine and started to drink again, gazing out across the rooftops towards the east where the shining river nudged deserted docks.

She knew she should stay calm, contact a headhunter, or that television producer in Gomborough, at least go through the motions of finding another job, but the Chablis stoked her sense of impasse.

The story would have got round. She knew the form. Marketing was a small gossipy world. There would be veiled references in the Trade Press, whisperings at Conventions.

She would always be the woman who blew her bubble.

At Fastfoods her name would be anathema. The Bubble was their symbol, their very totem. One does not prick the Product.

And while one may at length forgive the guilty, it is impossible to pardon the innocent.

But now she came to think of it, perhaps she was not entirely faultless after all. Had her heart really been in Nut Puffs from the beginning? Had she not been strangely distraite, unlike her old self? That label at the factory, hadn't she almost deliberately overlooked it? In former times, she'd have been on it like a beagle.

Was it mineral deficiency, character weakness or lack of conviction that was at the root of her late unevenness? As she poured the last glass from the bottle, she began to feel better, to see the thing more clearly.

Some plants, she thought, even under stone or concrete – shrivelled, seemingly extinguished – suddenly decide, or are switched on to decide, that they will not give up, they will push through to the light. So something by some mysterious alchemy had decided that she would no longer be subdued under a heavy lightless life of pushing meaningless morsels about in airtight sacs. Those feelings of responsibility of hers had been a sign. She saw it all now. Larry's words came back to her. They were all in airtight sacs. John Keats was an airtight sac. The whole city was an airtight sac.

The only thing she didn't quite know was: where was whatever it was that she was struggling upward from her airtight sac to reach? But perhaps that was the whole point. The plant doesn't know. Perhaps it was better it didn't. Because having once got up between the cracks in the concrete by dint of extraordinary exertion and effort, it was more than likely the poor bloody thing would get squashed to an atom by some great big bloody lorry.

'Poor old bloody dandelion,' she said. 'Probably better off spindly in the dark.'

The thing needed more wine for a detailed appreciation. But when she went away to the fridge for another bottle, to her irritation she found it was empty. She looked in the cupboard; still nothing. She recalled that she was to have collected more in the Porsche yesterday, but had other things on her mind.

The only drink she seemed to have in any quantity was a sticky liqueur she had brought back after a holiday in Turkey which tasted faintly of tomcats.

She finished the bottle and fell asleep.

When she woke up it was dark again and she felt sick.

171

She threw up and climbed back into bed again.

Next day she went out to get some dusty wine at the little store round the corner, and some dusty cans of food. She spent the day drinking, eating cold beans and watching old movies on the television.

Once she rang Poppy who sounded distant but it might have been the line.

'Come round, love,' said Poppy, 'but not Saturday.'

There seemed no point in going anywhere.

She went to bed, played with herself, drank again, watched television.

The telephone never rang.

She remembered the old woman down by the wilderness beside the river.

'It's the end of the world,' she said.

35

On the fourth day, she woke up with such a headache and in such a state that she didn't immediately open a bottle.

She tottered to the bathroom and looked at herself in the mirror.

A hag peered back; lank-locked, drawn-featured, pale and, as she now discovered, discernibly smelly.

She found aspirins, made coffee, took a bath, washed her hair and put on her make-up. She dressed carefully, choosing a demure grey suit and white silk blouse.

Looking at herself again, she found she was quite the old Charlet, apart from a certain puffiness around the eyes.

She guessed it must be the weekend. She would go and

see Poppy. If Poppy wasn't at home, at least she had the key. She would let herself in and stay for a while.

She had to get out of this place.

In the little carpark she used, she found the Porsche had been broken into and there were dents and scratches all over its front. She half expected to see a severed arm flopped beside the windscreen but there was none in evidence.

'No arm done,' she said to cheer herself up.

The stereo machine and all her cassettes had been removed.

She drove slowly with the wind wagging the torn canopy. She had always driven fast, to loud music, but now the sound of the wind and the engine refreshed her. The car, of course, would eventually go back to Fastfoods, but they couldn't have it yet.

She had some visits to make.

36

'Oh, love,' said Poppy, underlining the love. 'Oh LOVE, what pig's luck.'

She settled herself comfortably on the newly recovered sofa, and patted it for Charlet to sit down.

'Poor you,' she went on, 'you look terrible. What you must've been through. We were so worried about you. Have a drink?'

Charlet shook her head. Poppy nodded, too understandingly.

'I heard all about it from Bruce,' her friend continued. 'Poor Bruce. He was dreadfully upset.'

Charlet wondered momentarily if she were talking

about some other Bruce, but Poppy established it was indeed the Fastfoods one, with her next remark.

'I've picked up some of your other brands,' she said. 'I feel just dreadful about it, but it's good for the old career, though, isn't it? Bruce says it's just temporary, but who knows? I'm a bit inexperienced for full Brand Manager yet. But don't let's talk about me.'

Charlet let her go on talking about Poppy. She had noticed one of Bruce's special blazer buttons, something to do with an exclusive media-people's golf club, lying on the carpet just where she was sitting.

It was as evident a symbol of her friend's infidelity as a monogrammed contraceptive. Bruce always kept his blazer done up even in the ranker bouts of foreplay. The pressure on them, here in the sofa, must have been prodigious.

While Poppy babbled on – why had she never noticed how supremely self-interested her friend was? – hateful scenes kept coming to her mind, all the more hateful because she herself had enacted them on this same divan which Poppy had cribbed from the Waiting Room. Poppy guzzling like a hyaena, Bruce pumping like Arkwright's Mule.

It was almost as though he were there, sitting between them. She could hear their conversation.

'There. Wasn't that better than Charlet?'

'Oh yeah, yeah. Terrific.'

'She's coming here tomorrow, you know. I won't know how to look at her.'

'Who?'

'Charlet.'

'Let her stew. If she can't take a joke, she shouldn't sign on.'

'Do you think I'm awful?'

'Awful?'

174

Bruce would be pouring a drink now to get the taste of sex out of his teeth.

'Me being her best friend.'

'Everyone's their own best friend.'

'You used her, though, didn't you? There was something funny going on. We're not all blind. You're a shit really. You used her to get yourself off the hook.'

'You used her to get yourself on my cock.'

'That's different. All's fair in love . . .'

'And war, Poppy. Come on. You know the game.'

'I know the game, cock, and very well hung it is too.'

'That's enough,' said Charlet, 'enough, enough, enough.'

'What?' said Poppy, cut short in mid-analysis of her chances of getting the new bite-size poppadom snack. 'Well, I must say. I was only trying to cheer you up, take your mind off things.'

She suddenly spotted the blazer button, and swept it up off the floor as if it were a silly crumb. It was plain to see that she was guilty.

Charlet didn't hate her for it. She just couldn't stay there any longer.

'I mean, I have to go,' she said. 'There's a lot I have to do.'

'But you've only just arrived,' said Poppy, huffy because she was in the wrong.

'Things to fix, people to see,' said Charlet, wildly. 'Goodbye.'

She grabbed her handbag and walked to the door.

'Oh, love,' said Poppy. 'Do you really? Call you up soon. Must have lunch.'

Charlet had a vision of herself, a child again, running down the long corridor, opening doors on empty rooms.

Outside a drunk or madman or both, in a worn-out business suit, was pissing against a tree behind the garden wall, swearing furiously at the air, not even turning

175

with a fucking-cunting-buggering-twatting-arsehole as she passed.

They were trying to make her invisible.

37

She was invisible too to James when she telephoned from a callbox.

'I don't know you,' he said.

'Come on, James. It's Charlet.'

'Never heard of her.'

'We used to . . .'

'Can't say I recall. Are you the one with the big tits and the blue eyes? Or was it the other way round?

'It's Charlet, James.'

She now heard another voice in the background.

'Who's that?'

'Wrong number, I think,' said James.

'Wrong number my orifice,' said the voice. 'It's one of your girlfriends.'

'I keep telling you, I don't have any girlfriends.'

'Then what's all that about big tits? Give that to me,' and then, louder: 'Who is this? Speak up. I know you're there. I'll fucking kill you, big tits.'

Charlet put the telephone down. There seemed no future in the dialogue. James at least had not exaggerated his matrimonial problems.

She thought of calling Larry but changed her mind. The memory of that wrong she'd done him, that little bit of office avarice, made it impossible that she should turn to him now. Even if he shrugged off the offence, think nothing of it, Charlet, happens all the time, she'd not be able to forgive him for being so nice, and Harriet his new wife would look at her with big round owly eyes, ask her to stay and pounce at her with hot chocolate. It would be insupportable.

She called Larry anyway. A woman's voice answered.

'Hullo,' said Charlet. 'Is that Harriet?'

'No Harriet.'

The voice had a foreign accent. She tried again.

'Could I speak to Larry?'

'No Larry here.'

Charlet read out Larry's number.

'That's what you ring. No Larry here.'

'Do you know where he is?'

'He go north.'

'Do you know where?'

'Just north north. I not know. I took apartment from agent. They are so laze, they not give me number. In the all ways, I give you the number. But I no have number.'

Charlet waited a little just in case some sense might escape from the woman's language trap, but nothing emerging, she rang off. Her head was beginning to feel tight. At the same time, everything outside it – the trees, the people, the dog turds – seemed more and more like images, part of that vast back-projection which John Keats House had daily suggested.

She noticed she had put her foot in a back-projection, and wiped it abstractedly against the back-projection of her car wheel. She swayed and steadied herself against the fabric roof, looking round anxiously for cardboard policemen who might think she was still drunk.

She put her head in the car and headed at last for home.

Halfway there, she had another idea. She would call Martha. They hadn't seen each other since that lunch. There had been no communication. And as Charlet had become more and more involved with Nut Puffs, the friendship had dwindled to no more than a memory, a mere wisp of the past disintegrating in stormy weather. But it would be good to see Martha again. Martha would be substantial.

She stopped and called her.

'I need to see you,' she said.

'Fine,' said Martha, 'come on round. Trev's away. I've something to show you. Hurry now.'

Martha sounded odd, not in the least surprised that she should have called. But oddity, it seemed, was becoming the norm.

38

'How simply terrible for you,' said Martha.

For some reason, she was still in her négligé which kept slipping open to reveal Martha's long, flowerpot-like bosoms.

'The thing is,' said Charlet, trying to find something else to look at, 'everything seems to have come to an end. I've nowhere left to go.'

'But darling, you can come here. Trev left soon after I took my degree. I told you I'd been taking a degree? You must do it. You've simply got to take a degree. Well, Trev left. He couldn't take it.'

'The degree?'

'No, silly. Me with a degree.'

'Why was that?'

'I was a threat to him.'

Martha stuck out her breasts as if they would spike any man's guns.

'You were a threat?'

'Couldn't stand the competition, so he ran off with

that pigeon-brained waitress from the winebar, silly old noodle.'

'Oh dear.'

'I was relieved, to tell you the truth. It allowed me to discover my true self. I met this amazing woman.'

She has gone mad, thought Charlet.

'Did you know we're on a ley line here?'

'I didn't know that.'

'Ley lines are channels of energy. Feel.'

She took Charlet's hand and placed it on her left flowerpot. It wriggled under the emphasis of the gesture.

'You can sense it, can't you,' she continued. 'I'm charged. That's why I wear as little as possible. Clothes clog the essence. Why don't you take your clothes off?'

'I don't think I will if you don't mind,' said Charlet. 'The thing is, I'm rather at a loss in my life. You remember how we used to laugh about things? I needed a laugh. I know that's silly, and one can't laugh just like that, but I keep getting this feeling of absolute panic.'

'I know,' said Martha, 'me too. Take your clothes off.'

It was only by promising to return that evening to meet this amazing woman, that Charlet was able to get away.

39

The Makepeaces were playing a video game.

She had called in, not because she wanted to see them, but because she wanted to put off going home.

As soon as she glimpsed them through the window of the living-room, as she came up the path to the front door, she knew it was a mistake. They were crouching over the controls of the machine, hooting with mirth.

She started to turn back but they had seen her, and waved hectically.

'Come in, come in,' said Bobby, 'Caroline's making supper. Couldn't have come at a better moment. Drinky? We've just fixed our holiday plans. Brazil, we thought, this time with a week up the Amazon, see the rain-forests while they're still there. Down, Trotsky. And now we're playing zones.'

'Zones?'

'You know, Erogenous Zones. You have to get your tickle on to your opponent's whatsits. Your opponent meanwhile defending herself with an absolutely lethal hyper-slap. And, of course, vice versa. Rather the same as the old scoring system we used to have at University. You know. Breasts six, pussies ten. It's the latest thing, is Zones. Bloody expensive. The kids adore it. Plus ça change.'

They walked down the hall and went into the living room. The Makepeaces' two children were quarrelling excitedly.

'I touched her inside thigh. I did. Dad, tell her I touched her inside thigh.'

'You didn't. That was just my leg. So there.'

'Children, children. What does the scoreboard say?'

'It says 7.'

'That's an inside thigh, I'm afraid.'

'Oh, Daddy.'

The game continued at last. Bobby turned to Charlet, eyes candid with vacancy.

'Now, Charlet, let's get you sorted out.'

'I . . . it's hard to say.'

'Is it Howard? I gathered something was up.'

'It's . . . not just that . . .'

'Nipple, nipple,' the boy shouted.

'Quiet, Julian,' said his father.

'It's the end,' said Charlet. 'I've come to the end.'

'Our barrister friend liked you. I tell you. He really got the hots for you. Hold on, I'll call him up.'

'No,' said Charlet, 'I don't mean that. That's the last thing I mean.'

'Good heavens,' said Bobby, incredulously. 'What in the world *do* you mean? Down, Trotsky.'

'Clitoris,' screamed the child.

It was time to be on her way.

40

Still she drove on, unable to face the prospect of home.

Parking near the Precinct, she bought a ticket at the Classic, and watched a film about Swedish doctors making love in an old people's home.

Finally, she could put it off no longer.

It was dark when she arrived. She parked the Porsche a few yards away from the gate; an old instinct of evasion; you never knew what Howard might not have rigged up to spring at you if you were too obvious in your approach.

Tonight, there was something manifestly strange, though, about the place. Her perceptions strained through the Chinese lantern of her head. Ah yes, that was it. No lights.

She hurried forward, fishing for her keys, suddenly urgent, fearful. She gave a quick glance around her, up and down the road, at the dark shakiness of the trees, the hump-backed bushes.

The front door lock never opened unless you pushed, twisted and jiggled at the same time. She struggled away with the darkness breathing down her neck. Why did she always have this agony with keys?

The very sky, full of orange-grey flock clouds interlaced

with curlicues of the deepest orange-blue, seemed to press in upon her stiflingly like the walls of an inescapable Indian restaurant.

Fighting her intuitions of fear, she at last got the door to open, and stumbled into the darkened hall. As she did so, her senses conveyed something to her instincts that her reason could not take in. She opened her mouth in soundless astonishment.

The hall was empty. In the darkness, every stick of furniture seemed to have gone.

When the connections finally limped across her brain, neuron to neuron, like old men crossing a river, reminding her of her dream and confirming the reality, she gave a great sigh, uncertain whether to run back outside or to shut the door and lock out whatever it was that, most surely, was on its way.

But there really was no choice. She had to go forward. Besides, she told herself, this was not a nightmare, it was her home. Neglected, certainly; eccentric, undeniably; but as real as the stain on the wall where Howard had squirted the spider-web spray that had failed to spider-web.

She reached for a light switch, knowing that it wouldn't work, and clicked it to and fro, futilely.

Lit only by the moon shining between the flocky gaps of cloud, she struggled forward through the house, knowing there must be a simple explanation like spring-cleaning or refurbishment or some preposterous over-the-top Howardism, but at the same time haunted by she knew not what horrible possibility.

The kitchen, which she had half thought might be where they were all hiding surrounded by baking smells and cocoa cups, was as empty as the rest of the house. Somehow the absence of Howard's comfortable cooker, so permanent and gadgetful, was the worst indication of something irrevocable.

The telephone was still there on the wall, but of course it was dead.

Even the cupboard in the downstairs cloakroom was empty, all the old muddle of wellies and children's boots, cleaned out, wiped from memory.

She now forced herself to go upstairs.

The landing was empty. No table. No pictures. No rocking horse. Her own workroom, taken over by Pentelle, was also bare. No trace of desk or fashion plates. There was nothing in the spare room, nothing in the children's rooms. The very medicine cupboard with its cargo of old boracic bottles, menthol rubs, athlete's foot cream and superannuated talcs had been cleared from the bathroom.

There was a sound now. She recognized it, the moaning rasp of hot breath in a huge throat. It would be puffing at the door now, bulging the wood, padding into the hall, scenting her up the stairs, down the corridor, hot, implacable.

There was only one room left now, the bedroom she had shared with Howard. She knew now it would be useless, but she had to go in.

As she opened the door, the first thing she noticed was the bed. Thank God. There was something left after all. And weren't those suitcases standing beside it? It meant, after all, that the nightmare wasn't real. Howard might have left home, set up with Pentelle, all this did not matter, just so long as the thing didn't come.

But as she stood there, weak with relief, something horrible started to move on the bed.

A huge shape, white in the moonlight, started to rear and wave. Something primaeval, headless with eight legs, whimpering and mewing, writhing up at her.

Charlet screamed and fainted.

She woke up to Howard's wet face, mouthing at her.

'Hermione and I . . .'

He seemed to be talking about Pentelle, who was huddling on a wrap. Charlet struggled to adjust.

'Couldn't reach you . . . decided . . . finished . . . move out . . . her mother in hospital . . . big house . . . kids . . . your things attic.'

It was true. Almost everything in the house had been Howard's. She had told him she felt tied by possessions.

'Everything all right, sir?' said another voice. 'Sorry disturb, door open, keep eye house, didn't know still here.'

'Just clearing up. Wife bit of a shock. Be all right. Nothing serious.'

The policeman left. Pentelle started to apologize.

'Sorry, Charlet, honest. One of those things. Brandy?'

Charlet didn't say a word. Her face felt as if it had been carved in a Halloween pumpkin.

41

She drove fast because she knew there was a hurry. The old dream might be over, but she'd woken up in a new one. She had sometimes done that as a child, forcing herself to wake from a nightmare, finding herself in her familiar bedroom and then the horror starting to stir in the toy cupboard, beyond the curtains, underneath the table in the corner.

She knew, of course, that what she had seen, the monster on the bed, was Howard and Pentelle making love, soixante-neuf, the beast with two heads, or two sexes, the head and the sex fused, symbol of the times. She should not have been surprised, she thought. Sex was the national sport, the great rage.

It was all to do with Fastfoods. She knew that now.

They were adding ingredient 666 or was it 999 to every product they made, they were poisoning the environment with sex. Freddie had more or less blurted it out to her.

Those policemen had given her odd looks. Could it be that the Government was in on it? Instead of bread and circuses, it was snacks and sex. Altogether cheaper if just as messy.

And now they knew that she knew, they'd be out to destroy her.

There was just one place they wouldn't think of looking for her, one person she could turn to who would understand.

She took the motorway down to the river and followed the old dock road past the derelict mantis gantries locked forever in unanswered prayer, and on through the disused wharves and ruined warehouses.

Towards the end of the journey, though, she began to have trouble finding the way. Some of the streets she had marked on the previous trip seemed to have been wiped off the map. There were simply long lanes between desolations upon which dull fires smouldered.

Admittedly everything looked different at night, but this was something more.

She stopped, checked the street guide, drove on, turned a corner by a corrugated iron wall, and came up against the reason.

Huge machines filled half the street. They had already started to eat their way down the block.

Fearful that the monsters had already devoured the one place in the world that she now relied on, she hastily stowed the car down a little twisted alley that ran away from the street towards the river. A Porsche stuck out like a space craft in all this wilderness, and she didn't want it to be found just yet.

In the smoking darkness, half-lit by the guttering fires

and helped by the beam of her fading car-torch, she made her way towards the broken line of tenements.

Picking a path round blocks of fallen masonry, she stumbled past the sleeping engines, and checked the first doorway that was still intact.

Thank God, it was Number 29. They were still a little way off. He might yet be unharmed, sitting there in the darkness, staring at the wall, waiting for the interrogators to come, or dreaming fitfully of the green woods of his childhood.

If only she had come sooner! But somehow she knew that there had been no other way. It was decreed that now was the time. She remembered her mother trying to instruct her in the essence of Drama. There was a ritual to reconciliation that could not be short cut.

At last she was there. Number 47 sat squarely in the half-darkness, giving nothing away, not even a glimmer of reflection from its paneless windows.

She knew what she had to do.

Negotiating a broken railing, she went down the area steps, and gently tapped at the barricade of boards.

'Father,' she called, 'it's me, Charlet, your daughter. Don't be afraid. It's me.'

Putting down her torch on the parapet wall, she inched the barricade aside, revealing a doorway under the front steps. The door lay off its hinges, propped exhaustedly against the wall as if it had grown tired of the party but didn't know where else to go.

Beyond, there lay darkness.

She knew he would be in there.

'It's me, your daughter, Charlet,' she called again. 'Don't be afraid. I've come to take you home.'

Her torch was fading. She had to move quickly.

'Don't be afraid,' she called again. 'I'm coming in.'

Very cautiously she edged the door back a little so its

rusty hinges wouldn't snag her coat, and stepped under the lintel.

The weak yellow beams of her torch showed her the ruin of what had once been a kitchen. Blackened floorboards, showing here and there even blacker gaps where the planks had been burnt through, indicating that there had been a considerable fire down here at some point. An old-fashioned cast-iron stove still squatted under the chimneypiece, and a great cracked china sink with a couple of rusted taps stood in front of what had once been a window.

A spider scuttled across the chipped enamel and disappeared under the sediment of leaves and litter. Otherwise there was nothing else in the room.

In the far corner of the room, however, was another doorway – this time with its door still intact.

She called again to reassure him, tapping on the wood as if it were a hotel bedroom.

'It's me Charlet. May I come in?'

Still no response.

She opened the door which gave a sudden shocking owl-like screech, and peered in.

If the kitchen had been dark, this room was even dimmer, and, as she stepped under the lintel, she seemed to be enveloped in a darkness like the Plague of Egypt, her torch reduced to a glimmer that barely showed her hand. The air was stale as if in daylight it would be frosted with grease and decay.

There was still no sound. Making her way, inch by inch, around the wall – which she judged would be the safest part of the room if the floorboards were anything like their neighbours – she finally arrived at a roughly planked window which admitted the faintest hair-cracks of light from the distant fires. She started to pull at it. Even the faintest light was better than none. She could only manage to prise one plank off, but it served to reduce the absolute night.

She paused and looked round. Her torch, as if encouraged by the new source of illumination, managed a momentary surge of energy.

The combined flickering glow showed vague lumps on the floor which slowly revealed themselves as a vagrant's pathetically inadequate living essentials.

A kettle with a skew-whiff lid. A handle-less saucepan. Curious rolls of newspaper and felt which probably only survived because there was no use for them. A plastic pail without a handle. Half a hundred bottles.

And pushed against the furthest wall was a bigger mound altogether. A mound that weakly started to stir, and weakly flail its arms, and call out.

'Charlet. Is that . . . oh tell me . . . is that Charlet?'

She ran to him, crying with relief and amazement, kissing the poor sunken cheeks, drying the tears with her scarf.

Until now, half of her had known that he was unreal, merely her fantasy, a repository for unfulfilled hopes and emotions. She had hardly dared really to believe that he could still be alive, it was too important to her. That was why she had left it so long. And now he was indeed here to comfort her when the last door opened.

'I thought you wouldn't come,' he said.

'I knew you were here. I wanted to come but . . . Oh, why didn't I come before?'

'My little Charlet . . .'

'Why didn't you tell me? Get in touch with me?'

'You were so beautiful.'

And then he started to cough, great racking sounds that seemed to come from his stomach and threatened to crack the cockle-shell ribs.

'I must get you to a hospital,' she said, 'you shouldn't be in this place.'

She could tell by the sound of the coughing that he was very sick. But he started to struggle.

'Not hospital. Promise you won't send me to hospital. No more hospitals.'

She realized she'd made a mistake.

'It's all right. Promise. No hospital.'

She soothed him like a baby, the way she had never been able to soothe her own.

'It's all right. Rest. I'm here.'

'You're here. That's all that matters. Talk to me, Charlet.'

She paused, wondering whether to light a fire. It was deathly cold in there. But she decided that the smoke might make him cough still more. So she huddled closer to him under the greasy horsehair. His hand stroked her arm distractedly. There was so much she wanted to ask him.

'I have to know first,' she said, 'just a little about you. Where have you been? What have they done to you?'

'I was . . . in a hospital . . .'

She leant even closer to catch the whisper.

'. . . In the trees . . .'

'What was it? Why did they take you there?'

'There was something . . . I knew . . .'

His tired brain flickered like the firelight, struggling to remember. It was clear that he'd been tortured just as she imagined. She cursed herself for not doing something earlier, for being so engrossed in the bubble world; and the perversity of things that makes knowledge come too late.

Suddenly he spoke in a firm voice.

'It's the end, you know,' he said.

She'd heard that before somewhere. She imagined he was talking about himself.

'Don't worry,' she said. 'I'll get you out of here.'

'They won't let me go, you know. They'll catch me and then they'll . . .'

He was back in prison again, struggling.

'No . . . not the . . .'

'It's all right. I'm here. It's Charlet. You're safe.'

'It's in the water, you know,' he said piteously, looking up at her, and started to cough again.

He lay exhaustedly after the bout, full of words but voiceless.

'Don't talk any more,' she said.

They sat there in silence for several minutes, then suddenly he smiled up at her.

'Do you remember how you used to count when you were a tiny girl. One. . .two. . .ditt. You couldn't say three. And the garden? How you chased the cats? So green.'

Her mother had never mentioned such things. But, to quieten him, she began telling him about herself.

As she described her life, she was able to see it at last as a whole, whereas before it had been mere flashes of countryside, glimpsed through high hedgerows as through the chinks of a closed car. And, as she went on, she began to feel more and more ashamed. He had sacrificed his youth, his health, more or less his whole life – and others like him had done the same – and all she had done was play with bubbles. She hadn't glorified anything, made anything beautiful. She had splashed in the shallows and turned her back on the deeps. The fault was not merely in Fastfoods. Fastfoods was just a symptom. The fault was in herself. She had allowed, she had actively encouraged, the spider to eat the bright butterfly.

What had happened to her in the past few months was no more than justice.

She looked down on him as she talked to see if her own revulsion was echoed in his eyes, but he lay there smiling, nodding a little, the tears still wet on his cheeks.

Finally she stopped, thinking that at last he had fallen asleep.

But he stirred, opened his eyes, and smiled up at her radiantly.

'Oh Charlet,' he said. 'Oh Charlet. Wouldn't it be nice if something wonderful were to happen?'

She did not know quite what he meant, but she smiled back at him.

'It will,' she said. 'It will. We'll have such a time.'

And she started to tell him about where they would go, and what they would do. In a very little while, the tired old eyes closed again, and he was asleep.

She herself, at last, overcome by a great weariness, sank down beside him and they lay in the half-light of the fires on the waste, father and daughter, at last reunited in the sundering of sleep.

42

She woke with a start, uncertain how long she had slept.

For a moment, she thought she was on holiday again, in her student days. Lances of light from the broken boarding showed her the derelict room. Then she remembered.

She looked down at the wretched bundle of blanket and sackcloth that she'd slept on.

There was no sign of her father.

She started up, calling for him, beside herself with anxiety.

Then she was assailed by another memory. A grip of extraordinary strength – one arm around her body, and one round her neck – the struggle to free herself from the man she could not see, who said nothing, the hand over her mouth now, and the man on top of her, falling backwards, her clothes being torn, her breasts squeezed, the prolonged and reiterated rape, the darkness.

'Father,' she called again, but she knew he was dead.

She was half-naked, her breasts hurt, her lip was cracked, her legs were stained with blood. She was alone.

Instinctively, she pulled on the rest of her torn clothes.

There was a low noise outside like the premonition of an earthquake, the lamentation of the land. She shut her father's eyes. Pulled the blanket over his face. Walked across the ruined kitchen to the basement door, squeezed through the barricade, blinked at the sudden shock of the morning light.

The sky was full of clouds like smoke as though rising from the scene of a disaster.

She walked up into the street. She raised her eyes again and saw the buildings vulnerable as trees.

If she did not hold them together, they would fall apart, there would be nothing to stop everything falling apart. But, try as she might, she could not summon up the will to contain them. And slowly, very slowly, as she struggled to hold them together, the joists started to work loose in the masonry, the mortar turned to whirling dust, and bricks began flying through the air like leaves before the storm.

And she too at last was caught up and swept along in the universal dissolution.

PART TWO

'Thy hand, great Anarch, let the curtain fall,
And universal Darkness buries all.'

The Dunciad Alexander Pope

43

There you might think the story ends.

And, indeed, since we have nearly completed your course, and you will soon be going home to flash a perfect smile at the television cameras of your country's broadcasting service, you may have been growing understandably anxious that we would not reach an orderly conclusion before it was time for you to depart.

I can tell you are a stickler for order (otherwise you would not have wished to go through such a lengthy reconstructive undertaking).

Well, I am glad to have been able to relieve you on that score.

However, there are still a couple of deviant molars back there which will just give me time to administer one or two more twists to the tale before we can call it a day.

You found that scene with her father a little too sugary and Dickensian? So did I. It seems quite clear to me that she was simply raped by some vagabond. A horrible thing to happen to a girl who was already disturbed, and you can see why her subconscious would wish to invent a more heart-tugging version.

Would you care to rinse? Ah. You are admiring the new turquoise tint. I chose it myself. One gets so tired of ordinary blue.

Now let us to work. You will stop me, won't you, if it's hurting?

It was a Monday evening. I had just completed the

finishing touches to a rather neat little capping job, and was looking forward to leaving the office early. I had just bought a complete new set of the Mozart Piano Concertos which I wanted to start listening to.

As is my habit from time to time, I happened to glance out of the window and, yes, you have guessed. It was Charlet out there.

Dazed, bruised, dishevelled but still the woman I had been looking for all my life.

Clothilde had already gone. You are of course familiar with Clothilde, my nurse receptionist. She speaks little English but understands dentistry. I chose her for both qualities. Her accent is appalling, her comprehension of anything outside the compass of my activities limited in the extreme. I do not know what she is doing in this country. She looks on it with amazement, and the longer she stays the worse her command of the language. She looks like a smock-frocked gibbet, but she is an excellent person. However, enough of Clothilde.

I saw, as I say, this beautiful and distressed creature outside. She had as it were manifested from that alleyway you see, or rather you can't see but I can, opposite.

She stood there, swaying slightly, clutching at her torn coat, obviously looking for something – almost it seemed something in her head and not to be found in street or park – at any rate obviously lost.

I downed the tools I was putting away, and went down the stairs three at a leap.

To understand my emotions at this juncture it would perhaps help if I filled in a few details about myself with one or two scenes from my earlier life, since I begin to play a role in the story not simply as narrator but as one of the leads.

First, as you have occasion to know, I am a dentist.

It is in many ways a strange profession, neither exactly priest nor layman. People do not confide in their dentist the same way as they do, say, in their doctor. Indeed, very often they cannot do so since their mouths are obstructed, but that is not the only reason.

A dentist, like an undertaker, is a figure of fear. That is why there are so many jokes about them. But this is to some extent unfair. We are no more responsible for the inadequacies of nature's design than undertakers are for mortality. Can we even talk about Nature's 'design'? It is a chapter of accidents. Our teeth incorporate the very tale of our descent from ape to fruit-eating pithecus to hairy club-wielding carnivorous Magdalenian to smooth-tongued modern polyphage.

As we eat, we chew on a set of, as it were, oral compromises. No wonder our teeth need supervision. But that is not the fault of the dentist.

Again, my occupation emphasizes the worm-like nature of the human body. Mouth, tubes, fundament. Our lofty minds are attached to the Earth by vermiform coils. We are at the same time imprisoned and made possible by this hilarious arrangement. The paradox is constantly staring up at us, wagging its epiglottis.

Raise your hand if you need drainage.

Perhaps that is why dentists are often said to be so sexually active, this predominant concentration on an orifice through which passes the noblest expression of the spirit and the base nutrient of the flesh; every treatment is a penetration of a kind.

For myself, I am intrigued, sometimes even alarmed by the mouth. Indeed, it seems to me at times that I myself am in danger of being sucked down – the universe is full of holes – and that unless I stand very firmly and hold on to the back of the chair, so, I am going to fall down one of those colossal palpitating maws, luscious as a flytrap, fringed with its hard little petals of white teeth.

I mention these things since I know you are a thinking

person. I would not reveal such confidences to a mere cavity patient.

I am, I believe, less sexually than romantically impressionable – or perhaps an awkward combination of both.

I was married for some years to a small excitable woman who took on the role of a permanent residential critic; only my best was taken for granted, and my worst was never forgiven. Doubtless I fulfilled the same function for her. After some unfortunate scenes, we separated.

I took up with Penny later. Penny and I lived that sort of half-intimate, see you tonight if I'm not out with a client life, peculiar to capital cities and media people.

I know you will say that a dentist is not a media person, but what is this media they all talk about? Only a modern coinage for the organs of communication, and what could be more of an organ of communication than our old friend the mouth?

The mouth is my medium. I have a nice private practice; mainly actresses, businessmen, estate agents, wine merchants and yes, media people. Media people of the modern kind. Like yourself.

Penny and I had been together eight years. Any man would have been proud of her; she's a lovely creature, but I found I could not ask her to marry me. The excuse was that I'd been married before, have children, yes I have children, two sons, nearly grown up, don't want any more, had been worked to death.

'The thing is, love, I don't think you understand what a change having children makes to one's life. I'd marry you tomorrow but I know you'd want a child. I don't think I could take that again.'

She didn't believe me but was too proud to argue. She thought I didn't really want her. Perhaps this was true. We were held together by her dislike of change.

198

Occasionally she says she is going to buy her own flat and move out but she never does.

We lived together in my small house near the river. It is too small for someone as untidy as Penny. There were clothes, bits of make-up, pieces of jewellery everywhere. I hate the smell of leather in the bedroom, don't you? You get wafts in the night of dead animal.

But she always dressed superbly. It's a mystery to me how a woman can pick something here from a jumble in the cupboard, there from a pile under the bed, and here again from the mountain on her chair, and still look sleek and delicious to the outside world. That is the meaning of flair. But ultimately she is not for me.

Ever since I could remember, I had this feeling that somewhere out there was my perfect complement, waiting for me to find her, rescue her from the drab goblins, bring her up to daylight, the loved one of my heart – whom I would doubtless never meet.

I felt she was probably fair but it did not matter. The nose straight and short. The lip curving sweetly, neat and biteable as a lychee. The face oval, the eyes serious but bright, the brow candid, the mind full of interest and quirk.

Why did she not come forward? I sensed her so strongly lurking in the wings. She would have saved me so much time and foolishness.

'Where have you been? Behind what curtain were you from me hid so long?'

It would have been a kindness not to have been granted this vision at all; like being given a peep of Paradise, the perfection merely tormented.

I missed her every day; and though constantly disappointed in my search, there was something about the sight of unknown women that could madly rekindle my hopes.

I would rush past Clothilde in pursuit of this glimpse of

a sweep of hair from the window; a neatness of feature, the step graceful and yet springy as though the dull city pavement were lark-haunted wold.

'Just got to dash out,' I would call to Clothilde.

'Miss Gorringe vaits her abscess.'

'Won't be a minute. Haven't padlocked my bike.'

This last was an aside for Miss Gorringe. Clothilde knows I do not own a bicycle.

And down I would go rattling like a machinegun in my curiously clickety shoes, and the girl would be gone.

Of course, if I'd been lucky enough to have seen her parking her car, I would leave a note on the windscreen torn from my pad, gift of The Nenuphar Amalgam Company.

'I so much admired the finesse with which you parked, I felt quite undone. Please allow me to buy you a glass of champagne at Bertrand's, 7P.M., and show you my goldfish.'

I inserted the last bit because I know that girls have a tendency to trust men who love animals.

Returning, I would look up and see Clothilde watching me through the window. I would not feel ridiculous. One had to do these things.

Sometimes the fair one would show up, and for a heartpounding dinner or two, if I was lucky, the dirigible of romance would bounce along, lift a few feet into the air, and then flop back on to the ground again.

Penny used to say she liked me because I indulged her taste for woolly toys and talked to her turtle. She said I made silly sausage jokes. But was this not to miss my finer points?

I was becoming a little desperate. Where was the one beside whom all women were rehearsals, who would appreciate not just my silliness but my entirety? I was over forty, to put it mildly. She had better show her hand soon or she would find me a grave man. Already the hair in my ears was uncharmingly long, and the foliage in my nostrils given half a chance would be sprouting like seed-cabbage (I try to keep it under control for the patients' sake).

What a cruel stroke of Fate it is to give us these imaginings of perfection, and then to push hair up our noses.

Empedocles – I was given a classical education before turning to oral hygiene – Empedocles declared: 'Happiness is impossible, but we are condemned to search. That is the essence of Man's absurd predicament.'

Some search for it in their work, some in their children, some in the comforts of religion or the passionate rigmaroles of politics; and there are still some like me who against all the odds persist in looking for it in another person.

'No rest but the grave for the pilgrim of love . . .'

You have ruined my life, I thought; you, unknown, dear tormentor; filling me with a thirst for refreshment among these dry rocks. But no doubt, somewhere, in your way, you are searching for me too.

Such was the background to my bounding steps as I sprang down the stairway that fatal day, hastily checking my nose-hair, and out like a King's Messenger across the road.

One or two people were looking at the girl strangely as I made my own way over.

'Please,' I said, 'don't think me rude, but you look as though you might be lost.'

She lifted a face of the greatest sorrow to me, and said simply:

'More than that.'

'Oh come,' I said, stupidly jocular, 'it can't be all that bad.'

'Why not?' she enquired.

I could not answer her. I was tiptoeing with excitement

because I knew, as soon as she spoke, that this was indeed the person, dashed by what miracle of coincidence upon my shore, who would make all my foolishness sensible.

I had never met anybody with such a look of distance in the eyes. They were like the windows on a far country whose secrets I could not as yet perceive. I was at the same time shocked by her condition. It was plain to see that she had been in the wars.

'You are lost and appear distressed,' I said. 'May I offer you my hospitality? You need have no fear. I am a professional man.'

I did not like to say dentist in case she was put off.

She accompanied me upstairs without fear or expectation.

I let her into my waiting room where I made her a cup of tea using Clothilde's kettle which she had forbidden me to do as on one occasion I had broken it.

The girl sipped the brew as if it were nothing.

'Who are you?' I asked, 'and where did you get that cut on your forehead? I don't much like the look of it. Was it a car accident?'

She shook her head.

'I don't remember.'

'But who are you?'

'I don't know.'

'Do you remember nothing?'

She passed a hand wearily over her forehead.

'I'm sorry,' I said. 'I didn't mean to tire you with these questions. I think perhaps I should take you to a hospital.'

This seemed to agitate her.

'No. Don't do that.'

'Well, at least let me try to clean up these cuts of yours.'

She made no objection. I felt encouraged to explain my surgery.

'I am, as it happens, a dentist.'

She neither laughed nor flinched.

'We get a basic medical grounding,' I continued. 'Some people don't realize that.'

She evinced neither interest nor boredom. I busied myself swabbing her face. Once the dried blood had come away from the wound up by the hair-line, it proved in fact to be less of a cut than a graze on top of an ugly contusion.

There seemed to be brick-like red dust mixed up in the laceration. I decided that the blow had doubtless caused temporary amnesia. Had the world run so mad that it was starting to throw bricks at lovely women?

'If you don't want a hospital,' I said, 'I imagine you won't want to report anything to the police.'

'Not the police.'

She was quite adamant, but she couldn't tell me why.

'I'll have to watch you for a bit, then,' I said. 'You may have concussion.'

I took her pulse. It was, if anything, a little on the slow side. Her hands were fine and delicate without being neurotic. Her skin had a curiously exciting slippery-smooth texture like the film on a grape-pip.

'You don't feel sick?' I enquired.

She shook her head.

'Or drowsy?'

'No.'

I gave her one of Clothilde's mysterious Danish biscuits. She ate it without relish or revulsion.

'Somebody may be worried about you,' I said.

There was always the painful possibility that, after this, she might be another's. She wore no rings, though I thought I detected the ghost of a mark around the married finger.

I realized, in retrospect, that whoever had attacked her

had doubtless removed all her jewellery. But all she said was:

'I don't think so. I don't feel so.'

It was Mozart to my ears.

I felt a great wave of love for her, extraordinary for someone I had only just met. She was so vulnerable, and yet somehow so beyond distress.

'You can stay here as long as you like,' I said.

'Please don't let me delay you.'

'I have nothing to do that can't wait.'

'You're very kind.'

We sat for quarter of an hour. I gently took her teacup from her. She was holding it very tightly, and I knew how Clothilde values her china.

I offered her the use of the bathroom. She accepted, and I heard the shower running. She returned twenty minutes later looking greatly improved.

'That seems to have done the trick,' I said. 'Would you like me to look at your teeth?'

It seemed a way of passing the time. Besides, the inside of people's mouths can tell you a great deal about them.

For the first time, she gave the ghost of a smile.

'Do you always say that to women you find in the street?'

'I've known you all my life,' I said boldly.

She gave me a puzzled, again half-humorous look, and sat in the chair.

She had, inevitably, a near perfect set of teeth whose only flaws – a slight forward tilt of the canines and one gold inlay in the upper left molar – merely served to heighten the general impression of care and order. I wanted to jump in it straight away and pull the lid down. But I stifled these thoughts as being unworthy of her present condition.

I was also conscious of a faint sensation of guilt while I inspected her. I should really have had Clothilde in attendance while examining a female patient. In my profession, one cannot be too careful.

However, I was too carried away by love to let such considerations weigh.

Meanwhile, whatever emotions were surging in my breast, she seemed indifferent, simply closing her eyes and lying back in my chair, letting my hands touch the loveliness of her face while my suction-drainer goggled at her limpid trickles of saliva.

I lingered over my inspection, partly for my own pleasure, and partly because it seemed to soothe her. While I did so, a course of action was forming in my mind.

Night was falling. We could not remain in my surgery indefinitely. The girl seemed to have nowhere to go. Penny, by some kindness of the gods, was staying for three weeks with her sister in the north, who had just had a baby. The solution seemed obvious.

Concluding my investigation, I put my probe and spatula down, and helped her to her feet.

'Trust me,' I said. 'I'm going to take you to my house. You will be perfectly safe.'

She looked doubtful.

'You have my word of honour as a dentist.'

Suddenly she laughed. It was not a very happy laugh, but a laugh nonetheless.

'Is it a good word of honour?' she asked. 'Better than a pederast or a thief?'

'There are dentists doubtless who are both,' I replied. 'But there is a code of ethics.'

'There is honour among thieves.'

'So I have heard tell. But I must say I have yet to come across any.'

She laughed again, and started looking around the surgery.

'You'd need to be a thief to know, I suppose,' she said. 'Perhaps you are.'

Only of kisses, I wanted to reply, madly.

And then she shocked me.

'D'you keep any drugs here?' she asked.

Surely she wasn't that kind? All my dreams would have foundered on that. But she reassured me with her next remark.

'I just thought you might help me kill myself.'

'This is a cry for help,' I answered briskly.

'No. It is a cry for drugs.'

'They are all locked up and Clothilde keeps the key,' I lied.

'Do you know what?' she said. 'You make me laugh. You're nuts.'

And then she paused, looking puzzled at the word, as if at some time it might have meant something to her.

I didn't know whether she meant laugh at or with. I pretended to assume she meant with.

'Laughter's like pyrethrin,' I remarked lightly. 'It helps keep out the moths.'

She picked up my model skull and worked its jaws.

'Thus march we playing to our latest rest,
   Only we die in earnest, that's no jest,' she said.

She snapped the skull shut with a dreadful finality.

'You remember something at any rate,' I said.

I'm ashamed to say I was alarmed. I didn't want her waking up too quickly.

'Words not things,' she said. 'But maybe you're right. Perhaps it was the skull reminding me of something. And nuts for some reason.'

I could see I was going to have to watch her, and made a mental note to secrete my cashews when I reached home.

At any rate, she appeared to agree to my suggestion

that she accompany me, and I led her off down the stairs and across the street to the garage.

Suddenly she stopped.

'It's this place,' she said. 'There's definitely something funny about it. Like a postcard I've seen.'

My heart leapfrogged into my uvula. (This is a mistake many people make, incidentally. It doesn't come into the mouth. I have noticed it stops just short.)

'It's just another street,' I said, 'there's plenty more like it. Perhaps it reminds you of another one. But we can stay if you like. Or we can come back when you're rested.'

I was torn between humour and love like an eighteenth-century hero. Suddenly she folded up like a flower.

'Sorry,' she said. 'I'm so tired.'

44

So began the happiest days of my life.

The very first morning, after a good sleep (I put her, of course, in the spare room), she seemed physically much better.

I brought her breakfast in bed and I was glad to see her pick at the muesli with at least some semblance of appetite. She was so beautiful it made my senses spin. Beautiful, mysterious, elusive, dependent. I was, for the moment, her entire world.

'How's the head?' I asked, still anxious about possible concussion.

'Still on,' she said. 'I think I got a reprieve.'

Gallows humour, I thought, is better than none, but I made a note to lock up the aspirin. I use an electric razor. Anyway, she did not look like a wrist-slasher.

'Anything come back? Name? Rank? Number? Last known address?'

She shook her head.

'We'll have to call you something. Any suggestions?'

'Amnesia seems appropriate.'

She was henceforth known as Ammie. It had a waif-like ring to it.

'I have to go to work today,' I told her, 'but make yourself comfortable. I wouldn't do too much. Rest and get your strength back. Oh, and I wouldn't go too near the river.'

'Don't worry,' she said. 'I'm a coward in the water.'

'And whatever you do, don't go away.'

I rang her three times in the course of the day, but the telephone had been taken off the hook.

I was racked with anxiety. My hand shook. I made a hash of a perfectly straightforward cavity to the extent that Clothilde had to make a new batch of amalgam. She gave me some very odd glances.

The afternoon trudged by, and finally my last appointment was over. I couldn't wait to be off.

'Something got in wizz. Noodle pulpy,' said Clothilde, disapprovingly.

I left her to lock up and dashed home.

There she was in one of Penny's dresses, and looking even more delicious than the dinner she had made for us.

'Whose is this?' she asked, meaning the dress.

I told her about Penny. She made no comment. I poured her a drink, and asked her about her day.

She told me she'd spent most of it asleep. I chided her about taking the telephone off the hook, saying I'd been convinced she had wandered off somewhere and got herself lost, whether deliberately or not I hadn't fathomed.

Amnesiacs are terrible people to love. No name, no address, no phone number. Once gone, they're like water.

'You're crazy,' she said. 'Do you know that?'

Over dinner – roast duck from the freezer and orange soufflé – she asked me about my life. I told her what I could. It is difficult to describe what one knows too well. I was only interested in the present. The past was pointless.

However, I floundered through it for her amusement.

'I suppose you'll want to make love to me afterwards,' she said suddenly.

I was disconcerted, I admit it. It was true that the notion had been on my mind, but I had the feeling she was judging me.

'Certainly not,' I said. 'It would be an abuse of hospitality. Besides, you are in a sense my patient. I would not prescribe such a thing. It would be unethical. Perhaps you have a bad opinion of men? In my view, a minority give the rest of us a bad name. We are not all loud-mouthed, arrogant, domineering, and aggressive – but we are tarred with this brush because of the hooligan behaviour of the few.'

I could see her beginning to smile. That curiously cloaked mind of hers was the key to her love. I set myself to stroke it.

'The few, you say,' she replied. 'I should let women be the judge of that. Unfortunately I'm in no position to say since I've forgotten everything.'

'Sometimes, it's true,' I went on, 'it has seemed that women actually want us to behave in this loutish manner, since history is brimming with nice girls who have gone for brutes. Look, for instance, at the example of R. Z. Billson, who, despairing of ever mastering the gentler arts of persuasion, is reported to have stood on the corner of a certain fashionable street not far from here, and asked every woman of suitable age who passed whether they would like to go to bed with him. Certainly it is said that nine out of ten either slapped his face or gave some acid rejoiner, like "Get yourself a face transplant and come back next year," but rumour had it that one out of the ten accepted his invitation and followed him on the instant to his flat where he gave them the seeing-to of a lifetime.'

She gazed at me, amused, with raised eyebrows.

'I don't believe it,' she said.

'Neither, as it happens, do I,' I rejoined. 'First because R. Z. Billson is a particularly unpleasant media man with caries down to the roots, a face like a buttock, and too great a dependence for his bravado on the bottle. And, second, because this is exactly the sort of view of women propagated by the hooligan element.'

She was laughing now.

'You, of course, are different.'

'Yes of course. There are months when my gentle and considerate approach has not rated even one in thirty. Indeed, my experiences have sometimes tempted me to reflect that the prettier the woman the more likely she is to end up with louts because the sensitive and intelligent man – knowing that she has had a surfeit of offers – cannot bring himself to commit the cliché of making a pass at her.'

'Poor dentist.'

'However, I am resolutely optimistic, and since your slate has, as it were, however unfortunately, been wiped clean, perhaps we can regard my interest in you as genuinely original, and therefore to be taken with attention and sympathy.'

She let her hand rest lightly on my arm. There was a wealth of meaning in the gesture. We were pleased with each other that first evening. Everything seemed right.

Even the fact that we didn't sleep together drew us closer.

I think we were both nervous. I, because I had suddenly found, against all rational expectation, such extraordinary happiness and was afraid to bungle it with first-night ineptitude. And she . . . I could only surmise . . . because the very state of amnesia itself must have a worrying and tension-inducing effect upon the subject.It is difficult for a woman to give herself when she does not know who or what she is giving.

On the other hand, in certain circumstances, I believe some people would find that exciting. I could only wait and hope that so it would come to be for her.

I did not know much about the condition of amnesia. One does not wittingly have many cases in one's chair. Usually, one's patients are all too burdened with the circumstances of being themselves.

At any rate, I snatched an hour in my next lunch-break to leaf through a general textbook at the local library.

I gathered that it could be brought on by a blow. But equally it might be caused by mental stress and what is loosely called a breakdown, particularly among women.

If instinct falters in a woman, it can put a disproportionate strain upon the 'rational' or left-hand anterior lobe, and certain of the faculties of memory can suffer a temporary shutdown. This is what the books say.

45

Other people's love is like other people's pain. It is such a subjective matter.

I will not go into the details of our growing interdependence. It would be the ultimate act of desecration to bore you with a subject that I found so absolutely at my centre.

Believe me, it was so. I cannot explain it. I can only tell you. And at this stage, since there is only one molar to go, narrative is everything.

It began to seem to me that I too had lost my memory.

We were like children in a forest. Everything else was dark and gloomy, but in our clearing we had all we wanted. Light, food, shelter, warmth.

I began to grow impatient of the world's demands on my time. I was also more and more anxious, I must confess, that in town, surrounded by potentially familiar things, she might suddenly regain her memory and the spell might be broken – or at best that I would have to start, with what torments of uncertainty, all over again.

I had an idea.

'Let's go away,' I said to her. 'I've a holiday coming up. I'll advance it by a couple of weeks. We'll go to the Island of Old Empedocles himself. I've always wanted to look at that volcano. And the sea's warm and the wine's good.'

'Everything's a holiday at the moment,' she said. 'You don't have to take me away. I won't remember who I am, I promise. I never want to remember who I am. But I'd love to see the volcano.'

I obtained an amnesiac's passport for her – I had even thought of that.

It is incredible that bureaucracy should have a pigeon-hole for such a phenomenon, but there are apparently something like two thousand cases every year – a figure, I was told, that is on the increase – and at least five per cent of these have needed to travel for reasons of therapy.

I had the application countersigned by a medical friend of mine to whom I explained the case in nearly every particular.

He asked to see her, and I drove her over to his house.

He looked at her, at first cursorily, and said she appeared fit – apart of course from her memory loss – upon which he tested her but for which he could find no apparent cause. The bruise had nearly subsided. There was no sign of any lingering complication.

Then he asked her to undress so that he could give her a more thorough examination. I said, of course, that I would leave the room but she asked me to stay. She seemed not to want to be left alone with another man, even a doctor.

I knew it was going to be painful for me, but I could not do other than agree.

To see her unbutton her blouse, and shrug off her bra, so that the sweet breasts fell forward, and the nipples stiffened a little in the cooler air. To see her unzip her skirt, step out of her tights and panties, the legs so long and white up to the smallest outcrop of soft brown-gold hair through which I could see, for I could not tear my eyes away, the fragrant coombe of her sex. To see all this in the clinical light of the consulting room was to know a torment unsung by Virgil or Dante.

I was in such a state that I hardly heard him saying, at the end, that all seemed well, and that he positively recommended a change of scene. It might just jolt her memory when she returned.

I pulled myself together. I did not want him to note my distress.

I asked him how long amnesia usually lasted.

'It so much depends on its cause. It could be a day. It could be infinitely longer. Most of us have small temporary amnesias at some time or other. For instance, sometimes when we first wake up. You must have noticed it. On the other hand, a woman in Norway is reported to have had one that lasted seventy years.'

I prayed that this would be the case with Ammie.

'The fact is,' he went on, 'we still don't know very much about it. I'd be interested in seeing her again when you get back.'

I wanted to encourage his cooperation if not his case-histories, so I thanked him, and we were just about to leave when he said something else.

'You know you should report this, don't you?'

'I'm not taking her off against her will.'

'Certainly not,' agreed Ammie. 'I'd kick and scratch.'
She lifted a shapely shoe and gently prodded my leg.

'She has not been reported a Missing Person,' I
pursued.

It was true. I had checked. Giving a false name,
and pretending to be concerned about some fictitious
employee, I had enquired at the local police station.
There was no one remotely resembling her on their files.

My doctor friend gave up. I could see he thought there
was something going on but he couldn't quite tell what to
do about it. Besides, he was interested in keeping that
case-history to himself, at least for the moment, and that
was all we cared about.

I told Clothilde to postpone all my appointments – she
was terribly vexed and made violent guttural noises – but
I would hear none of it.

'I need a break, Clothilde,' I said. 'Enough of mouths.
I need to look down a bigger mouth than you can ever
show me.'

She looked at me as though I were mad and opened
her mouth obediently.

'Bidder mouse?'

'Mount Etna, my dear Clothilde. I'm going to the
island of Trinacria.'

46

Sicily was having a heatwave, unusual for that stage of
the season.

We stayed in a hotel on the beach, lay in the sun, swam,
ate fish, drank quantities of wine – Corvo, Rapitala, Etna

214

Rosso and Bianco – made little jokes about the few other guests and the waiters, looked at the Greek theatre at sunset, watched each other's eyes, held hands and kissed a great deal.

It doesn't sound an altogether original regime, but we felt we were the first people who had ever done it.

We were feeding on ambrosia.

We still did not make love. But I sensed, we both sensed, that the climate, both physically and emotionally, was right. It would happen. And when it did, I knew there could be no greater happiness for me under the moon. It was not a question of optimism. It was knowledge.

And then one day, one fateful and appalling day towards the end of our idyll, I decided it was time for us to take the trip to Etna.

The gods – who are still strong on the island – must have been jealous, for the excursion was our undoing.

The reason for my interest was primarily, of course, old Empedocles. As I have said, I studied the Classics as a boy, and had always been attracted to his story.

Empedocles – in case you are not familiar with the history of philosophy or the philosophy of history, whichever way you like to look at it – was a philosopher, poet and historian born in 493 BC in the Greek city-colony on Sicily of Agrigentum. He was a disciple of Telauges the Pythagorean, and warmly adopted the belief in the transmigration of souls.

He wrote a poem concerning his opinions on the various bodies that Nature had given him – girl, boy, lamb, bird, fish, and finally his own!

It is reported that he recited at the Olympic Games in rivalry with Hesiod and Homer.

The main tenet of his philosophy was that Love and Strife alternately rule the world, and that in the four elements there is always opposition and affinity.

This has always seemed to me to come nearer to an all-embracing picture of existence than many more sophisticated or 'spiritual' creeds.

Take the average human, a microcosm of the world. Do not Love and Strife vie in each one of us? Is not our eternal problem one of reconcilement? That is why we are bound to search for Happiness, the ultimate reconciliation, and never on this earth to find it.

Empedocles himself, believing perhaps that only the gods know true happiness, finally persuaded himself – with what disciplines and lucubrations we know not – that he had finally attained godhead. Indeed, he was revered as such in his city. No mean feat; for you know that prophets are not without honour save in their own country!

But he had failed so to instruct his body. And, growing old, he decided to cast himself into the crater of Etna so that his death should be unknown among men, and that his reputation as a god should survive – and possibly, with it, some essence of his godhead.

If this was so, the final irony was that his philosophy had the last word. In a final spirit of Opposition, the volcano, it is said, spewed out his sandal, by which it was known that his end had been mortal after all.

Or perhaps it was simply the contrary gods of the place.

47

The morning was perfect.

A light breeze fluttered by the flags, played arpeggios on the sheets of the beach dinghies, promising some cool respite on the long bus journey into the interior.

I watched her dress, enjoying the careless certainty which girls reserve for these functional but at the same time, to the lover, disturbing things of lace and lightness.

She knew that I was watching her, and turned to me tenderly, running a hand down herself.

'Dear heart,' she said, 'how like you this?'

I knew that we would be lovers that night.

The journey took us through those mysterious Sicilian villages and little towns which seem to have no reason for existence. You cannot imagine what anyone does there. And indeed there seem very few people around to do anything.

Even the bus was almost empty. It all served to heighten our sense of delicious isolation.

The great volcano came into sight round a bend, bigger than we had expected, with a plume of smoke at its summit. Our excitement mounted with the bus as it climbed gently upwards through endless fields of vines growing luxuriantly on the rich volcanic soil.

There is a god-like quality in most mountains, but particularly in this one – unpredictable, fire-breathing, mighty in history and legend.

The white vapour drifted gently from its top, two and a half miles high, and slid across to the southeast. Other smaller bonfire columns sprouted from lesser apertures a little further down, joining the lazy parent.

We had been told that on the southern flank the volcano was in a state of eruption, but it was quite safe for us to make the journey to the north side.

We hoped they knew what they were talking about. It made the whole undertaking just that little bit more piquant although, of course, we knew when we were together that we were inviolable.

Woods of oak and pine now replaced the vineyard terraces, and the bus moved up steeper foothills.

Finally, we arrived in a clearing that seemed to have

been transplanted from the Alps. Three or four log chalets, a small timber-mill and a pine-wrapped trattoria completed the scene. One half expected to see a ski-lift.

We descended from the coach, and it was suggested with that customary Italian attention to the priorities of life, that we should first have lunch. We would then complete the ascent in a four-wheel-drive 'autobus', a sort of extruded jeep which we could see across the yard.

We lunched upon prosciutto melone, piccata of veal, tomato salad and Etna Bianco. I remember the details of that lunch as though time itself had frozen the scene in Perspex and given it to me as a paperweight to place on top of all my other memories.

We ate on a terrace facing the trees, with the summit gently puffing above us, in a sheltered corner, on a pink and white chequered tablecloth. The bread, I remember, was remarkably good – not the usual Italian stuff baked with chalk. A single old thrush seemed to share our appreciation. We threw it crumbs which it gobbled like a python.

Somewhere a boy whistled 'La donna e mobile'. An old woman knitted in the sun. A faint smell of wood-smoke, that inevitable companion of Alpine scenes, mixed fragrantly with the food.

'I never want to be anywhere but here,' she said.

At last it was time to go. We collected battered anoraks from an old guide who issued them from his hut.

'Fa molto freddo,' he smiled, looking up at the summit and handing us each a pair of sooty boots into the bargain. 'Sono per le ceneri nere . . . il Duca di Wellington.'

It was clearly a joke he had made before, and intended to remind us to add a gratuity, but we smiled at him as if it were fresh minted.

They fitted appallingly and smelt.

Holding hands, we took our places in the three-quarters empty autobus, our only companions an elderly pair of

Germans, a woman who looked like a French school-teacher (but what was she doing here in term-time?) and a brace of youths who talked non-stop in a language we could not trace, all the way to the summit and quite possibly down again.

The wrinkled guide accompanied us; but as he could not speak a word of English and none of us appeared to have more than restaurant Italian, his guidance seemed to be of purely token value.

The bus surged forwards. We were on our way.

Climbing more comfortably if less decorously than the Sage, we reached the end of the tree-line in five minutes or so. It was touching to see the way the trees wavered, thinned, and finally gave up the struggle. One or two hung on, fools or rebels, nestling lingeringly in dips and folds. And then they too fell away.

There was still foliage left, sparse grasses and succulents of a sort. But on the ground in between them and, now, above, we began to see the true nature of the majestic mountain.

It was the biggest slagheap in the world.

Its constituent parts were unvarying clinker.

The bus ground on. The plants too became thinner. We had temporarily lost sight of the summit, and lurched upwards through a blackened wilderness. We played a game of who could see the last vestige of vegetation.

I had thought it had been a stubborn little squidge of indeterminate red-green that had taken up residence under the shelter of a bare black bank, but we turned another corner, and she pointed.

A small alpine fumitory was clinging to a sooty ledge as if its life depended upon it, which of course it did.

'It's like saying goodbye to a friend,' she said.

Indeed, it was like the end of life itself. Nothing else moved up here.

No bird, no insect, no cat-a-mountain or scorpion; only the immortal gods and insolent humans.

It was really becoming quite alarming.

Great patches of the clinker had fallen away in landslides. Fissures began to abound, some of them emitting smoke; lazy and menacing. We could see where the track had been repeatedly diverted, where old paths disappeared over new precipices.

'I hope the driver knows what he's doing,' I murmured, a faint presentiment beginning to gather in my stomach.

The danger didn't seem to worry her a bit.

'Terrible climb for an old man,' she said.

I had forgotten Empedocles.

'I think he got it wrong, though,' she continued. 'It's more like hell than heaven. In an exciting sort of way, I mean.'

She put her hand on mine. She didn't want me to think she wasn't enjoying it.

Finally the bus stopped. We got out.

The cloud must have started to gather as we drove. Intermittent patches of mist sped above us. We shivered, thankful for the anoraks and smelly boots.

The guide pointed upwards and started to walk.

Suddenly, in the silence punctuated only by the low ruffles of the wind, the mountain proclaimed itself.

Boom. Boom.

She shivered again.

'Come on,' I said, 'let's stay in the bus. No need to go to the top. We won't see anything with this cloud. It'll be cold.'

But she wouldn't listen.

'We've got to go and see old Empedocles,' she said. 'There's something up there.'

'Probably just a smelly old boot,' I told her.

We trudged after the guide, who was indicating that we

should follow him exactly. He seemed to be leading us into the heart of nothingness.

The cloud played with us, now closing thickly around us, now lifting and showing us dunes of cinder, high as hills, which we were traversing.

The air was thin at this height, and we were panting a little. The noise of the god grew louder.

Boom. BOOOM.

She paused, looking puzzled.

I wanted to take her back there and then, but we would never have found the path on our own in all that cloud, and the thought of losing our way among the smoking desolation was enough to override any other fears.

And so we followed on.

At long last, after climbing the steepest slagheap yet, the slope eased and we found the little party gathering near the edge of a vast overhanging lip. The old German woman had sat down and was being tended by her husband. They both looked distinctly grey. But then, as I looked around, we all did. The mountain had the effect of taking all colour from everything.

The vapour swirled about us, making us look like characters in some heroic Victorian lithograph, all tattered flags, fainting women, and gestures.

'Pericoloso,' said the guide, standing on the very edge of the lip. 'Cratere di Etna.'

Presumably, I thought, he knows what the lip is made of. There could have been no way up if it had broken.

Below, we could see but a fraction of the vast central bowl of the volcano, a scree-strewn cliff sloping precipitously downwards. Indeed, I reflected, as the cloud closed in cutting off even this glimpse, Empedocles or no Empedocles, we could have been standing on any foggy cliff-top just about anywhere.

Then suddenly, as if to refute me, the giant spoke again.

Boom Boom BOOOOM.

And a great blast of hot wind made us all step backwards involuntarily, expecting heaven knew what rattling bombardment of pumice, fires, sulphurs and brimstone.

I was ashamed of my fears when I saw her still standing, poised like Empedocles himself, upon the brink.

I went up to her and took her arm.

'You're as fearless as the Philosopher,' I said. 'I'm afraid the forces of Nature temporarily overcame my sense of History.'

Nervousness always makes me donnish. The mountain roared again.

Boom Boom Boom BOOOMPH.

This time I forced myself not to step back. Once again the blast struck our faces.

She turned to me a face terrible in its awakening.

'Oh my God,' she said. 'Nut Puffs.'

I had no idea what she meant. She trembled on the very lip of the overhang. I reached out to her.

'Let me go,' she said. 'I've had enough of this.'

I held her fast. The guide looked at us strangely.

On the way back down that terrible mountain, she began to tell me her story, the distance opening between us like the earth itself.

Epilogue

Once you have tasted the heights, it makes the mere world seem like a particularly nasty basement.

The tragedy of life is not what happens but what might have happened.

So it was with us. The angel with the flaming sword, or the guardian spirit of Etna, or the old fart of a Philosopher, had turned us out of our secret garden.

It made us cross with each other.

When we reached our hotel, she had finished her tale.

I poured her a drink.

She began taking her clothes off.

'Come on,' she said. 'We may as well screw. You've waited long enough.'

She said it so cruelly that I agreed.

It was an intensely pleasurable but joyless coupling. Her body was affinity. Her mind strife.

Afterwards, she filled in certain details of her story that I was particularly puzzled by. Marketing was a closed book to me. Would that I could have left it in that happy state.

Whether or not her narrative was truthful in every particular, I cannot say. Certain parts of it, especially the sexual emphasis, the pheromone subplot and the sections relating to her father, struck me as being tinged by fantasy. On the other hand, the main burden of the tale has unmistakable overtones of truth. And it is even instructive to note that a vociferous group of wholefood enthusiasts recently created something of a stir by claiming that, in Fastfoods' corporate logo, one could find unmistakable symbols, if not of diabolism, at least of pagan ritual.

At any rate, she had more courage than me. On our return, trying to hang on to the shreds of happiness, I suggested to her that we could still work something out, that I still loved her.

She smiled and went upstairs.

She is probably up there at this minute.

I still feel, given time, she may come down. She may indeed. Yes I am convinced of it.

There.

Your teeth are finished.

You can return to your country and smile without constraint. Look in the mirror. You have nothing to hide.

Would you care to rinse? The lilac tint is proving popular.

On with your coat. So.

The nurse will show you to the stair.

I am numb at the moment, but the feeling will return.

Should you have further problems, do not hesitate to get in touch.